Alfred John Church

# The Story of the Iliad

With Illustrations after Flaxman (Edition 2)

Alfred John Church

**The Story of the Iliad**
*With Illustrations after Flaxman (Edition 2)*

ISBN/EAN: 9783744749565

Printed in Europe, USA, Canada, Australia, Japan

Cover: Foto ©Andreas Hilbeck / pixelio.de

More available books at **www.hansebooks.com**

# THE STORY OF THE ILIAD

BY THE

REV. ALFRED J. CHURCH, M.A.

*Sometime Professor of Latin in University College, London*

*With Illustrations after FLAXMAN*

SECOND EDITION

LONDON

SEELEY AND CO., LIMITED

ESSEX STREET, STRAND

1895

THE GODS DESCENDING TO BATTLE.

# PREFACE

Fourteen years ago, in introducing my 'Stories from Homer' to the public, I expressed the hope that they would 'represent Homer not unfaithfully to readers, old and young, who did not know him in the original.' The book has found, on both sides of the Atlantic, many such readers, and not a few, I am proud to think, who, knowing the original, have judged this adaptation to be not altogether unworthy of it. If I could have anticipated so warm a welcome for my little work—the sale now exceeds twenty thousand copies—I should not have attempted to compress into a single volume the substance of the two poems. The two volumes which I

now publish, under the titles of ' The Story
of the Iliad,' and ' The Story of the
Odyssey,' give a much fuller, and, I trust,
a more adequate presentment of them.
In the first of these the narrative has
been made continuous and completed by
a beginning and an ending, both very
brief, and containing, it may be said,
nothing that is not strictly Homeric; in
the second, Homer's own order has been
restored, so that Ulysses now tells his
adventures in the first person.

A. C.

# CONTENTS

# CONTENTS

# LIST OF ILLUSTRATIONS

# THE STORY OF THE ILIAD.

## CHAPTER I.

### OF WHAT BEFELL BEFORE THE QUARREL.

LEDA, the wife of Tyndareus, King of Sparta, bare a daughter, Helen by name, that grew to be the fairest of all women upon earth. She married Menelaüs, son of Atreus, and for a while dwelt in peace with her husband, bearing him a daughter, Hermioné by name. But there came to the court of Menelaüs, who was by this time King of Sparta, a certain Paris, second in birth among the sons of Priam, King of Troy. Him did Menelaüs hospitably entertain, but Paris repaid his kindness with evil, for he carried off his wife, the fair Helen, and took with her many of the King's possessions.

Then Menelaüs, with his elder brother Agamemnon, who was over-lord of all the

Greeks, went to all the chiefs, and prayed that they would help them to avenge this wrong. Thus was a great host gathered together, even a hundred thousand men, and eleven hundred fourscore and six ships. At Aulis in Eubœa was their gathering; and from Aulis they crossed over to Troy.

The great chiefs of the host were these:—

First the two brothers, the sons of Atreus.

Next Diomed, the son of Tydeus, and with him Sthenelus.

Nestor, son of Neleus, who had outlived three generations of mortal men.

Ulysses, son of Laertes, from Ithaca.

Thoas the Ætolian.

Idomeneus, King of Crete, and Meriones with him.

Tlepolemus, son of Hercules, from Rhodes.

Eumelus, son of Admetus and Alcestis, from Thessaly.

And, bravest and strongest of all, Achilles, and with him Patroclus.

For nine years did the Greeks besiege the city of Troy. They prevailed, indeed, in the field, but could not break through the walls.

Now because they had been away from their homes for many years, they were in want of things needful. Therefore it was their custom to leave part of the army to watch the city, and with part to spoil the cities in the country round about. And in this way the great quarrel that caused such trouble to the host came about.

## CHAPTER II.

### THE QUARREL.

The Greeks sacked the city of Chryse, where was a temple of Apollo, and a priest that served the temple. And when they divided the spoil, they gave to King Agamemnon, with other gifts, the priest's daughter Chryseïs. Thereupon there came to the camp Chryses, the priest, wishing to ransom his daughter. Much gold he brought with him, and on his staff of gold he carried the holy garland, that men might reverence him the more. He went to all the chiefs, and to the sons of Atreus first of all, saying:—

"Loose, I pray you, my dear daughter, and take the ransom for her; so may the gods that dwell in Olympus grant you to take the city of Troy, and to have safe return to your homes."

Then all the others spake him fair, and would have done what he wished. Only Agamemnon would not have it so.

"Get thee out, graybeard!" he cried in great wrath. "Let me not find thee lingering now by the ships, neither coming hither again, or it shall be the worse for thee, for all thy priesthood. And as for thy daughter, I shall carry her away to Argos, when I shall have taken this city of Troy."

Then the old man went out hastily in great fear and trouble. And he walked in his sorrow by the shore of the sounding sea, and prayed to his god Apollo.

"Hear me, God of the silver bow! If I have built thee a temple, and offered thee the fat of many bullocks and rams, hear me, and avenge my tears on these Greeks with thine arrows!"

And Apollo heard him. Wroth was he that men had so dishonoured his priest, and he came down from the top of Olympus, where he dwelt. Dreadful was the rattle of his arrows is he went, and his coming was as the night when it cometh over the sky. Then he shot the arrows of death, first on the dogs and the mules, and then on the men; and soon all along the shore rolled the black smoke from the piles of wood on which they burnt the bodies of the dead.

For nine days the shafts of the god went throughout the host; but on the tenth day Achilles called the people to an assembly. So Hera bade him, for she loved the Greeks, and grieved to see them die. When they were gathered together he stood up among them, and spake to Agamemnon.

"Surely it were better to return home, than that we should all perish here by war or plague. But come, let us ask some prophet, or priest, or dreamer of dreams, why it is that Apollo is so wroth with us."

Then stood up Calchas, best of seers, who knew what had been, and what was, and what was to come, and spake.

"Achilles, thou biddest me tell the people why Apollo is wroth with them. Lo! I will tell thee, but thou must first swear to stand by me, for I know that what I shall say will anger King Agamemnon, and it goes ill with common men when kings are angry."

"Speak out, thou wise man!" cried Achilles; "for I swear by Apollo that while I live no one shall lay hands on thee, no, not Agamemnon's self, though he be sovereign lord of the Greeks."

Then the blameless seer took heart, and spake: "It is not for vow or offering that Apollo is wroth; it is for his servant the priest, for he came to ransom his daughter, but Agamemnon scorned him, and would not let the maiden go. Now, then, ye must send her back to Chryse without ransom, and with her a hundred beasts for sacrifice, so that the plague may be stayed."

Then Agamemnon stood up in a fury, his eyes blazing like fire.

"Never," he cried, "hast thou spoken good concerning me, ill prophet that thou art, and now thou tellest me to give up this maiden! I will do it, for I would not that the people should perish. Only take care, ye Greeks, that there be a share of the spoil for me, for it would ill beseem the lord of all the host that he alone should be without his share."

"Nay, my lord Agamemnon," cried Achilles, "thou art too eager for gain. We have no treasures out of which we may make up thy loss, for what we got out of the towns we have either sold or divided; nor would it be fitting that the people should give back what has been given to them. Give up the maiden, then, without conditions, and when we shall have taken this city of Troy, we will repay thee three and four fold."

"Nay, great Achilles," said Agamemnon, "thou shalt not cheat me thus. If the Greeks will give me such a share as I should have, well and good. But if not, I will take one for myself, whether it be from thee, or from Ajax, or from Ulysses; for my share I will have. But of this hereafter. Now let us see that this maiden be sent back. Let them get ready a ship, and put her therein, and with her a hundred victims, and let some chief go with the ship, and see that all things be rightly done."

Then cried Achilles, and his face was black as a thunder-storm: " Surely thou art altogether shameless and greedy, and, in truth, an ill ruler of men. No quarrel have I with the Trojans. They never harried oxen or sheep of mine in fertile Phthia, for many murky mountains lie between, and a great breadth of roaring sea. But I have been fighting in thy cause, and that of thy brother Menelaüs.  Naught carest thou for that.  Thou leavest me to fight, and sittest in thy tent at ease.  But when the spoil is divided, thine is always the lion's share.  Small indeed is my part — 'a little thing, but dear.' And this, forsooth, thou wilt take away!  Now am I resolved to go home.  I have no mind to heap up goods and gold for thee, and be myself dishonoured."

And King Agamemnon answered: "Go, and thy Myrmidons with thee!  I have other chieftains as good as thou art, and ready, as thou art not, to pay me due respect; and Zeus, the god of council, is with me.  I hate thee, for thou always lovest war and strife.  And as for the matter of the spoil, know that I will take thy share, the girl Briseïs, and fetch her myself, if need be, that all may know that I am sovereign lord here in the host of the Greeks."

Then Achilles was mad with anger, and he thought in his heart, "Shall I arise and slay this caitiff, or shall I keep down the wrath in my breast?"  And as he thought he laid his hand on his sword-hilt, and had half drawn his sword from the scabbard, when lo! the goddess

Athené stood behind him (for Hera, who loved both this chieftain and that, had sent her), and caught him by the long locks of his yellow hair. But Achilles marvelled much to feel the mighty grasp, and turned, and looked, and knew the goddess, but no one else in the assembly might see her. Terrible was the flash of his eyes as he cried: "Art thou come, child of Zeus, to see the insolence of Agamemnon? Of a truth, I think that he will perish for his folly."

But Athené said: "Nay, but I am come from heaven to abate thy wrath, if thou wilt hear me; white-armed Hera sent me, for she loveth and cherisheth you both alike. Draw not thy sword; but use bitter words, even as thou wilt. Of a truth, I tell thee that for this insolence of to-day he will bring thee hereafter splendid gifts, threefold and fourfold for all that he may take away. Only refrain thyself and do my bidding."

Then Achilles answered: "I will abide by thy command for all my wrath, for the man who hearkens to the immortal gods is also heard of them." And as he spake he laid his heavy hand upon the hilt, and thrust back

ATHENE SUPPRESSING THE FURY OF ACHILLES.

the sword into the scabbard, and Athené went her way to Olympus.

Then he turned him to King Agamemnon, and spake again, for his anger was not spent: " Drunkard, with the eyes of a dog and the heart of a deer! never fighting in the front of the battle, nor daring to lie in the ambush! 'Tis a race of dastards that thou rulest, or this had been thy last wrong. But this I tell thee, and confirm my words with a mighty oath — by this sceptre do I swear. Once it was the branch of a tree, but now the sons of the Greeks bear it in their hands, even they who maintain the laws of Zeus; as surely as it shall never again have bark, or leaves, or shoot, so surely shall the Greeks one day miss Achilles, when they fall in heaps before the dreadful Hector; and thou shalt eat thy heart for rage, to think that thou hast wronged the bravest of thy host."

And as he spake he dashed the sceptre, all embossed with studs of gold, upon the ground, and sat down. And on the other side Agamemnon sat in furious anger. Then Nestor rose, an old man of a hundred years and more, and counselled peace. Let them listen, he said, to his counsel. Great chiefs in the old days, with whom no man now alive would dare to fight, had listened. Let not Agamemnon take away from the bravest of the Greeks the prize of war; let not Achilles, though he was mightier in battle than all other men, contend with Agamemnon, who was sovereign lord of all the hosts of Greece. But he spake in vain. For Agamemnon answered : —

" Nestor, thou speakest well, and peace is good. But this fellow would lord it over all; yet there are some, methinks, who will not obey him. For if the immortal gods have made him a great warrior, do they therefore grant him leave to speak lawless words ? Verily he must be taught that there is one here, at least, who is better than he."

And Achilles said: " I were a slave and a coward if I owned thee as my lord. Not so: play the master over others, but think not to master me. As for the prize which the Greeks gave me, let them do as they will. They gave it; let them take it away. But if thou darest to touch aught that is mine own, that hour thy life-blood shall redden on my spear."

Then the assembly was dismissed. Chryseïs was sent to her home with due offerings to the god, the wise Ulysses going with her. And all the people purified themselves, and offered offerings to the gods; and the sweet savour went up to heaven in the wreathing smoke.

But King Agamemnon would not go back from his purpose. So he called to him the heralds, Talthybius and Eurybates, and said : —

" Heralds, go to the tents of Achilles, and fetch the maiden Briseïs. But if he will not let her go, say that I will come myself with many others to fetch her; so will it be the worse for him."

Sorely against their will the heralds went. Along the seashore they walked, till they came to where, amidst the Myrmidons, were the tents of Achilles. There they found him, sitting between his tent and his ship. He did not rejoice to see them, and they stood in great terror and shame. But he knew in his heart wherefore they had come, and cried aloud: " Come near, ye heralds, messengers of gods and men. 'Tis no fault of yours that ye are come on such an errand."

Then he turned to Patroclus (now Patroclus was his dearest friend) and said: "Bring the maiden from her tent, and let the heralds lead her away. But let them be witnesses, before gods and men, and before this evil-minded King, against the day when he shall have sore need of me to save his host from destruction. Fool that he is, who knoweth not to look back and to look forward, that his people may be safe!"

Then Patroclus brought forth the maiden from her tent, and gave her to the heralds. And they led her away; but it was sorely against her will that she went. But Achilles went apart from his comrades, and sat upon the seashore, falling into a great passion of tears, and stretching out his hands with loud prayer to his mother, Thetis, daughter of the sea. She heard him where she sat in the depths by her father, the old god of the sea, and rose from the gray sea, as a vapour rises, and came to where he sat weeping, and stroked him with her hand, and called him by his name.

"What ails thee, my son?" she said.

Then he told her the story of his wrong, and when he had ended he said:—

"Go, I pray thee, to the top of Olympus, to the palace of Zeus. Often have I heard thee in my father's hall, boast how, long ago, thou didst help him when the other gods would have bound him, fetching Briareus of the hundred hands, who sat by him in his strength, so that the gods feared to touch him. Go now, and call these things to his mind, and pray him that he help the sons of Troy, and give them victory in the battle, so that the Greeks, as they flee before them, may have joy of this king of theirs, who has done such wrong to the bravest of his host."

And his mother answered him: "Surely thine is an evil lot, my son. Thy life is short, and it should of right be without tears and full of joy; but now it seems to me to be both short and sad. But I will go as thou sayest to Olympus, to the palace of Zeus; but not now, for he has gone, and the other gods with him, to a twelve days' feast with the pious Ethiopians. But when he comes back I will entreat and persuade him.  And do thou sit still, nor go forth to battle."

Meanwhile Ulysses drew near to Chryse with the holy offerings.  And when they were come within the haven, they furled the sail, and laid it in the ship, and lowered the mast, and rowed the ship to her moorings.  They cast out the anchor stones, and made fast the cables from the stern.  After that they landed, taking with them the offerings and the maid Chryseïs.  To the altar they brought the maid, and gave her into the arms of her father, and the wise Ulysses said : " See now ; Agamemnon, King of men, sends back thy daughter, and with her a hundred beasts for sacrifice, that we may appease the god who hath smitten the Greeks in his wrath."

Then the priest received his daughter right gladly, and when they had ranged the beasts about the altar, and poured out the water of purification, and took up handfuls of bruised barley, then the priest prayed, " Hear me, God of the silver bow! If before thou didst hearken to my prayer, and grievously afflict the Greeks, so hear me now, and stay this plague which is come upon them."

So prayed he, and the god gave ear.

Then they cast the barley on the heads of the cattle, and slew them, and flayed them, and they cut out the thigh-bones and wrapped them up in folds of fat, and laid raw morsels on them. These the priest burned on fagots, pouring on sparkling wine; and the young men stood by, having the five-pronged forks in their hands. And when the thighs were consumed, then they cut up the rest, and broiled the pieces carefully on spits. This being done, they made their meal, nor did any one lack his share. And when the meal was ended, then they poured a little wine into the cups to serve for libations to the gods. After that they sat till sunset, singing a hymn to the Archer God, and making merry; and he heard their voice and was pleased.

When the sun went down they slept beside the stern-cables; and when the dawn appeared then they embarked, raising the mast and spreading the sail; and Apollo sent them a favouring wind, and the dark blue wave hissed about the stem of the ship as she went: so they came to the camp of the Greeks.

But all the time Achilles sat in wrath beside his ships; he went not to the war, nor yet to the assembly, but sat fretting in his heart, because he longed for the cry of the battle.

# CHAPTER III.

## THE ASSEMBLY.

WHEN the twelfth day was come, Thetis rose out of the sea, and went to high Olympus. There she found Zeus sitting apart on the topmost peak of Olympus, and she knelt down before him; with her left hand she clasped his knees, and with her right she took his beard, and she made her supplication to him.

"O Father Zeus, if ever I have aided thee by word or deed, fulfil now my prayer. Give honour, I beseech thee, to Achilles my son, that hath so short a space of life; for now Agamemnon hath put dishonour upon him, taking away the gift that the Greeks gave him. Grant, therefore, that the men of Troy may prevail for a while, so that the Greeks may do honour to my son."

So she spake, but Zeus sate long time silent; but Thetis would not loose her hold.

Then she spake again: "Give me now thy promise, and confirm it with a nod, or else deny me. So shall I know that I am held least in honour of all the gods."

Then Zeus made answer much disturbed: "This is a hard matter, for thou wilt set me at strife with Hera, and she will upbraid me with bitter words. Even now she is ever reproaching me, saying that I favour the men of Troy in the battle. Therefore do thou get thee away, that she know not of thy coming; and I will consider how this thing may be best accomplished. And now I will assure my promise with a nod; for when I give my nod, then the thing may not be repented of or left undone."

So he spake, and nodded with his dark brows, and the hair waved about his head, and all Olympus was shaken.

Then Thetis departed, diving into the deep sea, and Zeus went to his own house, and all the gods rose up before him. And when he sat upon his chair, then Hera, knowing that Thetis of the silver feet had held counsel with him, addressed him with bitter words.

"Who hath been in counsel with thee, thou plotter? Thou dost always take pleasure, when I am absent, in secret devices, and never tellest thy thought to me freely."

To her the sire of gods and men made reply: "Hera, think not to know all my thoughts; that were too hard for thee, even though thou art my wife. That which is fitting thou shalt hear first; but into such counsel as I take by myself inquire thou not."

Hera answered: "What sayest thou? I have not pried into thy counsels. These thou devisest as thou wilt. And now I sorely fear that Thetis of the silver feet hath prevailed with thee. At dawn of day I saw her kneeling before thee; thou hast granted, I doubt not, that Achilles shall have honour, and that many of the Greeks shall die beside their ships."

To this Zeus made reply: "Verily nought escapeth thee, thou witch. If it be as thou sayest, such is my will. Do thou sit silent, and obey. Else all the gods in Olympus shall not save thee, when I lay upon thee the hands that none may stay."

Then Hera was afraid, and held her peace, and all the gods were troubled. But Hephæstus the craftsman spake, saying: " This indeed will be a grievous business, if ye two come to strife for the sake of mortal men, and make trouble among the gods. If such ill counsels prevail, what pleasure shall we have in our feasting? Now will I advise my mother that she make peace with Zeus, lest he rebuke her again. Were he minded to hurl her from these seats, who should withstand him?"

Thereupon he put the double-handled cup into his mother's hand, and said: " Have patience, mother, for all that thou art vexed, lest I see thee beaten before mine eyes. I could not help thee. Once before, when I would have succoured thee, he grasped me by the foot, and flung me from the threshold of heaven. All day I fell, and at sunset I lighted in Lemnos."

Then Hera smiled, and took the cup from her son. And he went round to all the gods, going from left to right as a cupbearer should, and poured the nectar from the mixing-bowl, and laughter without end was woke among the blessed gods, when they saw the Haltfoot go puffing through the hall.

So they feasted in the hall, lacking neither the lyre, for on this Apollo played, nor singing, for the Muses sang sweetly, answering one to the other.

Gods and men slept that night; but Zeus slept not, for he thought in his heart how he might do honour to Achilles. And as he thought, he judged it best to send a deceiving dream to Agamemnon. Therefore he said: "Go, deceiving Dream, to the swift ships of the Greeks, and seek the tent of Agamemnon. Bid him make haste and arm the Greeks, for that he shall of a surety take the city of Troy."

So the dream went to the tent of Agamemnon, and found him wrapped in sleep. It took the shape of Nestor, the old chief, whom the King honoured more than all besides.

Then the false Nestor spake: "Sleepest thou, Agamemnon? It is not for kings to sleep all through the night, for they must take thought for many, and have many cares. Listen now to the words of Zeus: 'Set the battle in array against Troy, for the gods are now of one mind, and the day of doom is come for the city, and thou shalt take it, and gain everlasting glory for thyself.'"

And Agamemnon believed the dream, and knew not the purpose of Zeus in bidding him go forth to battle, how that the Trojans should win the day, and great shame should come to himself, but great honour to Achilles, when all the Greeks should pray him to deliver them from death. So he rose from his bed, and donned his tunic, and put over it a great cloak, and fastened the sandals on his feet, and hung from his shoulders his mighty silver-studded sword, and took in his right hand the great sceptre of his house, which was the token of his sovereignty over all the Greeks.

First he called a council of the chiefs by the ship of King Nestor; and when they were seated, he said: " Hear me, my friends. This night a dream came to me in my sleep; most like it was to Nestor. Above my head it stood, and said: ' Thou sleepest, son of Atreus. It is not for kings to sleep all through the night. Now mark my word; I come to thee from Zeus, who careth for thee, though he be far away. He bids thee call the Greeks to battle, for now thou shalt take the city of Troy.' So spake the Dream. Come, therefore, let us rouse the Greeks; but first I will try their spirit, counselling them to flee to their homes, and do ye dissuade them."

Then up rose Nestor in his place, and spake: "Had any other told us this dream, we had thought it false; but seeing that he hath seen it who is chief among us, let us call the people to arms."

Then the heralds made proclamation, and the people hastened to their places. Even as the bees swarm from a hollow rock and cluster about the flowers of spring, and some fly this way and some that, so the many tribes marched from the ships and the tents to the place of the assembly. Great was the confusion and great the uproar, and nine heralds sought to quiet the people, that they might listen to the speaking of the Kings; and at the last the Greeks ceased from their shouting, and sat in their places.

To them Agamemnon rose up, holding the

sceptre in his hand, and spake thus: "O my friends, ill hath Zeus dealt with me. He promised me that I should take the city of Troy, and so return to my home. But his words were deceitful, for now he bids me go back to Argos, inglorious, having lost much people. Shame indeed were it for men to know hereafter that we who are so many have yet fought in vain; many we are, and we fight with them that are fewer than ourselves, and yet we see no end. Verily, if the Greeks and the men of Troy should make a truce and number themselves, and the Greeks should be ranked in tens, and for each ten should take a man of Troy to pour the wine, verily, I say, many a ten would lack a cupbearer. Fewer indeed by far are the Trojans, but they have allies, valiant spearmen, who hinder me from taking the city. And now nine years have passed, and the timbers of our ships are rotted, and the rigging is worn; and our wives and our children sit at home and wait for us. Come, therefore, let us flee to the land of our fathers, for Troy we may not take."

So spake the King, and stirred the hearts of the people; that is to say, of all that knew not his secret counsel. All the assembly was moved as the sea is moved, when the east wind raiseth the waves, or as a cornfield, when the strong west wind comes upon it, and shakes the ears Shouting they hasted to the ships, and laid hands on them to drag them down, and some made clear the launching channels, and drew the shores from under the sides.

Then had the Greeks returned, even though fate willed it not. But Hera spake to Athené: " Will the Greeks thus idly flee to their homes ? and will they leave Helen a boast to Priam and to Troy, Helen, for whom so many have fallen far from their fatherland? Hasten now, and turn them from their purpose."

So Athené hastened down from Olympus, and she found Ulysses, who had laid no hand upon his ship, for grief had touched him to his heart. To him she said: "Son of Laertes, will ye indeed flee to your fatherland, and leave Helen, for whom so many have fallen, to be a boast to Priam and the men of Troy? Go now, and dissuade the Greeks, and suffer them not to drag their ships to the sea."

And when Ulysses heard the voice of the goddess, he cast away his cloak, and ran. King Agamemnon gave him his sceptre, and, bearing that, he went among the ships. When he saw a chief, he said with gentle words, " Hold, sir, it ill becomes thee to be a coward; sit still and hold the people back. Thou knowest not the mind of the King; he did but make trial of the spirit of the Greeks. Anger him not, lest he do some mischief to the people."

But when he saw a common man, he smote him with his sceptre, and said: " Fellow, sit still, and listen to them that are better than thou. Let there be one master, one king, to whom Zeus has given authority."

Thus did he turn them from their purpose. And they hasted again to the assembly with such a noise as when a wave breaks along the shore.

But, when all the rest were silent, Thersites alone flouted and jeered the princes, that he might move laughter among the Greeks. Most ill-favoured was he of all that came to Troy, bandy-legged, and halting on one foot, with a hump on his back, narrow-chested, and his head misshapen, with straggling down thereon. Loud he shouted now, reviling Agamemnon : —

"What lackest thou yet, son of Atreus? Full of bronze are thy tents, and many the fair women whom we have given thee for a prey. Wantest thou more than these? Surely a leader of men should not bring the Greeks into trouble. And ye, who are women rather than men, why sail ye not home, and leave this man to gorge himself with his spoils alone? For now he hath wronged Achilles, taking away his gift — Achilles, who is far better than he. Surely Achilles is mild of temper, or this, son of Atreus, had been thy last wrong-doing !"

Thereupon Ulysses rose up beside him, and spake in wrath: " Peace, babbler ; take not the name of kings upon thy lips, nor taunt thy betters. Hearken now to me : if I hear thee speak idle words again as thou hast done this day, surely I will strip from off thee cloak and tunic, and drive thee to the ships with shameful blows." So speaking, he smote him with the sceptre on back and shoulders ; and a bloody weal rose up beneath the blow. All dazed, the fellow cowered down and wiped away his tears.

Merrily laughed the others, saying one to his neighbour: "Often hath Ulysses done well, but never better than now, when he hath stopped this babbler's tongue. He will not rail against the kings again."

Then Ulysses stood up to speak, holding the sceptre in his hand; and Athené stood by his side, in the likeness of a herald, bidding the people keep silence that all, nearest and farthest alike, might hear his words.

"Now, O King," he said, "the Greeks go about to shame thee, abiding no more by their promise which they made thee coming from Argos; to wit, that they would not return till they had taken the city of Troy. Truly there is toil enough here to make us sick of heart and wishful to return. For a man will feel weary if he be kept but a single moon from his wife by winter winds and stormy sea, and we have lingered here for twelve moons nine times told. But it is not well to tarry long and come back empty-handed, after all. Ye all remember — all whom death hath not carried away — what befell in Aulis when the host was gathered to make war on Troy, and we were sacrificing to the immortal gods under a fair plane tree by a spring, — ye remember, I say, how a great serpent, fiery red and horrible to behold, glided from beneath the altar, and darted to the tree. There on the topmost bough was a sparrow's brood, crouching beneath the leaves. Eight were they in all, and the mother was the ninth. These the serpent devoured, one by one, twittering piteously; and the mother flew around, crying for her children. Her last he caught by the wing, twisting himself about. And when he had devoured the brood and the mother, the god that sent him made the sign yet more manifest, turning him into stone. Then Calchas said, as we stood wondering: ' Why are ye silent? It is to us this portent hath been sent. As the snake hath eaten the brood of eight and the mother the ninth, so for nine years shall we make war in the land whither we go, and in the tenth we shall take the fair city of Troy.' So he spake; and, without doubt, his words shall be fulfilled. Remain, therefore, ye Greeks, till ye have taken Priam's mighty town."

So he spake, and all the Greeks shouted in assent; and the ships sent back the shout as it had been thunder.

Then King Agamemnon stood up, and said: "Go now to your meal, and afterwards we will join the battle. Let every man whet well his spear, and fit his shield, and feed his horses abundantly, and look to his chariot, that all day long we may fight, and cease not, even for a little space, till, haply, night shall come and separate the hosts. Truly the band of the shield shall grow wet, and the hand be weary that holdeth the spear, and the horse shall sweat that draweth the polished car. And whoso holdeth back from the fight, tarrying at the ships, nothing shall save him from feeding the dogs and the fowls of the air."

Then the Greeks shouted again. Quickly did they scatter themselves among the ships and the tents, and make their meal. And Agamemnon made a feast, and called thereto the chiefs, Nestor and Idomeneus, and Ajax the Greater and Ajax the Less, and Diomed, and Ulysses; but Menelaüs, good at need, came uncalled, knowing that he would be welcome.

Then King Agamemnon stood up and prayed: "O Zeus, let not the sun set and the darkness fall before I humble Priam's roof-tree in the dust, and burn his doors with fire, and rend the coat of Hector on his breast!"

So he prayed, but Zeus hearkened not as yet.

And when the feast was ended, the chiefs marshalled their hosts for the battle; and Athené in the midst swept through the host, urging them to the conflict; and in every heart she roused delight of battle, so that there was no man but would have chosen war rather than to return to his home. As is the flare of a great fire when a wood is burning on a hill-top, so was the flash of their arms and their armour, as they thronged to the field. And as the countless flocks of wild geese or cranes or swans now wheel and now settle in the great Asian fen by the stream of Caÿster, or as the bees swarm in the spring, when the milk-pails are full, so thick the Greeks thronged to the battle in the great plain by the banks of the Scamander.

# CHAPTER IV.

### THE DUEL OF PARIS AND MENELAÜS.

So now the hosts drew near to battle. With many a cry the men of Troy came on, clamorous as a flock of cranes when they fly southward from the winter and the rain. But the Greeks marched in silence, resolute to stand by one another in the battle; and beneath their feet rose up a great cloud of dust, thick as the mist which the south wind brings over the mountain-tops — the mist which the shepherd hateth, but the thief loveth more than night.

They were now about to fight, when from the ranks of the Trojans Paris rushed forth. He had a panther's skin over his shoulders, and a bow and a sword, and in either hand a spear, and he called aloud to the Greeks that they should send forth their bravest to fight with him. But when Menelaüs saw him he was glad, for he said that now he should avenge himself on the man who had done him such wrong. So a lion is glad when, being sorely hungered, he finds a stag or a wild goat; he devours it, and will not be driven from it by dogs or hunters. He leapt from his chariot and rushed to meet his enemy; but Paris was afraid when he saw Menelaüs, and fled back into the ranks of his comrades, just as a man steps back in haste when unawares in a mountain glen he comes upon a snake. But Hector saw him, and rebuked him: "Fair art thou to look upon, Paris, but nothing worth. Surely the Greeks will scorn us if they think that thou art our bravest warrior, because thou art of stately presence. But thou art a coward; and yet thou daredst to go across the sea and carry off the fair Helen. Why dost thou not stand and abide the onset of her husband, and see what manner of man he is? Little, I ween, would thy harp and thy long locks and thy fair face avail when thou wert lying in the dust! A craven race are the sons of Troy, or they would have stoned thee ere this."

Then Paris answered: "Thou speakest well,

Hector, and thy rebuke is just. As for thee, thy heart is like iron, ever set on battle; yet are beauty and love also the gifts of the gods, and not to be despised. But now set Menelaüs and me in the midst, and let us fight, man to man, for the fair Helen and for all her possessions. And if he prevail over me, let him take her and them and depart, and the Greeks with him, leaving you to dwell in peace; but if I prevail they shall depart without her."

Then Hector was glad, and going before the Trojan ranks, holding his spear by the middle, he kept them back. But the Greeks would have shot at him with arrows and slung stones, only Agamemnon cried aloud and said, " Hold, Hector has somewhat to say to us."

Then Hector said: " Hear, Trojans and Greeks, what Paris saith, Paris who hath bred this quarrel between us : ' Let all besides lay their arms upon the ground, and let Menelaüs and me fight for the fair Helen and all her wealth. And let him that is the better keep her and them, but the rest shall swear faith and friendship.' "

Then Menelaüs stood up and spake: "Listen

to me, for this trouble toucheth me nearer than you all. The Greeks and the men of Troy would fain, I think, be at peace, for they have suffered grievous things because of my quarrel and of the wrong that Paris did. Therefore we two will fight together, and let him perish that is doomed to die. Bring two sheep, ye men of Troy, a white wether for the sun, and a black ewe for the earth, and we will bring another for Zeus. And because the sons of Priam are high-handed and light of faith, let Priam himself come, and do sacrifice, and take the oath. Young men are ever changeable; but when an old man is among them, he taketh thought for all."

So spake Menelaüs; and both the armies were glad, hoping to see an end of doleful war.

Then Hector sent a herald to the city, to summon Priam to the sacrifice and to fetch the sheep.

And while he went, Iris, in the guise of Laodicé, fairest of the daughters of Priam, came to Helen, where she sat in her hall, weaving a great web of double breadth and dyed with purple, whereon she had wrought many battles of the Greeks and the men of Troy. Iris came near and said: "Come, dear sister, and behold this marvel. Heretofore the Greeks and the men of Troy have fought together on the plain, but now they sit in peace, and the war is stayed; for Paris and Menelaüs are to fight for thee, and thou shalt be the wife of him that shall prevail."

So spake the goddess, and roused in Helen sweet longing for her former spouse, and her city, and her parents. So she wrapped herself in white apparel, and went forth from her chamber, weeping the while.

Meanwhile Priam sat on the wall with the old men. They had ceased from war, but in speech they were to be admired; they were like to the crickets that sit upon a tree in the wood, and send forth a thin, sweet voice. And as they talked, the fair Helen came near, and they said: "What wonder that men should suffer much for such a woman, for indeed she is divinely fair! Yet let her depart in the ships, nor bring a curse on us and our children."

But Priam called to her: "Come near, my

daughter, that thou mayest see him that was thy husband, and thy friends and kinsmen. I find no fault with thee, for 'tis not thou, 'tis the gods who have brought about all this trouble. But tell me, who is this warrior that I see, so fair and strong? There are others even a head taller than he, but none of such majesty."

And Helen answered: "Ah, my father! I owe thee much reverence; yet would that I had died before I left husband and child to follow thy son. But as for this warrior, he is Agamemnon, a good king and brave soldier, and my brother-in-law in the old days."

"Happy Agamemnon," said Priam, "to rule over so many! Never saw I such an army gathered together, not even when I went to help the Phrygians when they were assembled on the banks of the Sangarus against the Amazons. But who is this that I see, not so tall as Agamemnon, but of broader shoulders? His arms lie upon the ground, and he is walking through the ranks of his men just as some great ram walks through a flock of sheep."

"This," said Helen, "is Ulysses of Ithaca,

who is better in craft and counsel than all other men."

"'Tis well spoken, lady," said Antenor. "Well I remember Ulysses when he came hither on an embassy about thee with the brave Menelaüs. My guests they were, and I knew them well. And I remember how, in the assembly of the Trojans, when both were standing, Menelaüs was the taller, but when they sat, Ulysses was the more majestic to behold. And when they rose to speak, Menelaüs said few words, but said them wisely and well; and Ulysses — you had thought him a fool, so stiffly he held his sceptre and so downcast were his eyes; but as soon as he began, oh! the mighty voice, and the words thick as the falling snow! No man then might vie with Ulysses, nor thought we any more of his outward appearance."

Then Priam said, "Who is that stalwart hero, so tall and strong, overtopping all by head and shoulders?"

"That," said Helen, "is mighty Ajax, the bulwark of the Greeks. And next to him is Idomeneus. Often has Menelaüs had him as his guest in the old days, when he came from Crete. As for the other chiefs, I see and could name them all. But I miss my own dear brothers, Castor, tamer of horses, and Pollux, the mighty boxer. Either they came not from Sparta, or, having come, shun the meeting of men for shame of me."

So she spake, and knew not that they were sleeping their last sleep far away in their dear fatherland.

Meanwhile the heralds were bringing the sheep from the town, and wine in a goatskin; and Idæus, the herald, carried a bowl and golden cups. He came near to King Priam, and told him how the armies called for him. So he went, and Antenor with him. And he, on the one side, for the Trojans, and King Agamemnon for the Greeks, made a covenant with sacrifice that Paris and Menelaüs should fight together, and that the fair Helen, with all her treasures, should go with him who should prevail.

And when the sacrifice and the prayers were ended, King Priam said: "I will go back to Troy, for I could not endure to see my son fighting with Menelaüs. But which of the two is doomed to death, Zeus and the immortal gods only know."

So he spake and climbed into his chariot and took the reins; and Antenor stood beside him; so they went back to Troy even as they came.

And afterwards Hector and Ulysses marked out a space for the fight, and Hector shook two pebbles in a helmet, looking away as he shook them, that he whose pebble leapt forth the first should be the first to throw his spear. And it so befell that the lot of Paris leapt forth first. Then the two warriors armed themselves, and came forth into the space, and stood over against each other, brandishing their spears, with hate in their eyes. Then Paris threw his spear. It struck the shield of Menelaüs, but pierced it not, for the spear point was bent back. Then Menelaüs prayed to Zeus: "Grant, Father Zeus, that I may avenge myself on Paris, who has done me this wrong; so shall men in after time fear to do wrong to their host." So speaking, he cast his long-shafted spear. It struck the shield of Paris and pierced it through, and passed through the corselet, and through the tunic, close to the loin ; but Paris shrank aside, and the spear wounded him not. Then Menelaüs drew his silver-studded sword and struck a mighty blow on the top of the helmet of Paris, but the sword broke in four pieces in his hand. Then he cried in his wrath, " O Zeus, most mischief-loving of the gods, my spear I cast in vain, and now my sword is broken." Then he rushed forward and seized Paris by the helmet, and dragged him towards the hosts of the Greeks, for he was choked by the band of the helmet. And truly he had taken him, but Aphrodité loosed the strap that was beneath the chin, and the helmet came off in his hand. And Menelaüs whirled it among the Greeks and charged with another spear in his hand. But Aphrodité snatched Paris away, covering him with a mist, and put him down in his chamber in Troy. Then Menelaüs looked for him everywhere, but no one could tell him where he might be. No son of Troy would have hidden him out of kindness, for all hated him as death.

Then King Agamemnon said, " Now, ye

sons of Troy, it is for you to give back the fair Helen and her wealth, and to pay me, besides, so much as may be fitting for all my cost and trouble."

So spake King Agamemnon, and the Greeks applauded.

# CHAPTER V.

### THE BROKEN OATH.

MEANWHILE the gods sat in council in the hall of Zeus; and fair Hebe poured out for them the nectar, and they pledged each other in cups of gold, looking down upon the city of Troy. Then spake Zeus, seeking to provoke Hera with taunting words: —

"Two helpers hath Menelaüs among the goddesses, even Hera and Athené. But now they sit still and take their pleasure, while Aphrodité walketh beside Paris, and delivereth him from instant death. Yet, seeing that Menelaüs hath prevailed, let us consider what shall next be done. Shall we stir up war again, or make peace between the hosts? If it please you to make peace, then let Menelaüs take Helen to his home again, and let Priam's city continue."

So he spake. But Hera and Athené sat wrathful side by side, meditating evil in their hearts against the men of Troy. Athené kept silence, for all the fury that raged within her, but Hera could not contain her wrath, and spake : —

"What is this thou sayest, son of Chronos? Wouldst thou make void all my toil and trouble, with which I have gathered this people together, that Priam and his sons may be destroyed? Do as thou wilt; but it pleaseth not the other gods."

To her Zeus spake in answer wrathfully: "Tell us what evil have Priam and the sons of Priam done in thy sight that thou desirest so pitilessly the downfall of this fair city of Troy? Verily wert thou to pass within the gates, and eat Priam raw, and his sons with him, then might thy hate be satisfied. Do, then, as thou wilt. Let not this matter breed ill-will betwixt me and thee. Yet remember what I say. If I be minded to destroy in time to come some city that thou lovest, say me not nay, nor hinder me, for in this have I yielded to thy will, though sore unwilling. Verily of all the cities of men that lie beneath the stars, I have loved holy Troy the best. Never there has my altar failed of feast and banquet and the sweet savour that is the due of gods."

Then Hera answered: "Three cities have I that I love, Argos and Sparta and Mycenæ. If they have offended thee, destroy them; I begrudge them not; nor, indeed, could I withstand thy will. Yet my toil also should not be made vain; for I, too, am a daughter of Chronos, and first in place among the immortals, seeing that I am thy wife, who art the King. Come, therefore, let us yield to one another, and the other gods will follow us. Let now Athené go down, and bring it to pass that some one of the Trojans begin the strife and break the truce."

Thus she ended, and Zeus said not nay, but spake straightway to Athené: "Make haste, get thee down to the host, and bring it to pass that the men of Troy break the truce."

So Athené sped down from the top of Olympus, like to a star which Zeus sends as a sign to sailors on the sea, or to some host that goeth forth to battle; and wonder cometh upon all that behold it.

Among the host of Troy she went, taking

upon herself the shape of Laodocus, son of Antenor, and went to Pandarus, son of Lycaon, where he stood among his men. Then the false Laodocus said: " Pandarus, darest thou aim an arrow at Menelaüs? Truly the Trojans would love thee well, and Paris best of all, if they could see Menelaüs slain by an arrow from thy bow. Aim then, but first pray to Apollo, and vow that thou wilt offer a hundred beasts when thou returnest to thy city Zeleia."

Now Pandarus had a bow made of the horns of a wild goat which he had slain; sixteen palms long were the horns, and a cunning workman had made them smooth, and put a tip of gold whereon to fasten the bow-string. And Pandarus strung his bow, his comrades hiding him with their shields. Then he took an arrow from his quiver, and laid it on the bow-string, and drew the string to his breast, till the arrow-head touched the bow, and let fly. Right well aimed was the dart, but it was not the will of heaven that it should slay Menelaüs. For the daughter of Zeus stood before him, and turned aside the shaft, waving it from him as a mother waveth a fly from her child when he lieth asleep. She guided it to where the golden clasps of the belt came together, and the breastplate overlapped. It passed through the belt, and through the corselet, and through the girdle, and pierced the skin. Then the red blood rushed out and stained the white skin, even as some Lycian or Carian woman stains the white ivory with red to adorn the war-horse of a king. Even so were the thighs and legs and ankles of Menelaüs dyed with blood.

Sore dismayed was King Agamemnon to see the blood; sore dismayed also was the brave Menelaüs, till he spied the barb of the arrow, and knew that the wound was not deep. But Agamemnon cried: "It was in an evil hour for thee, my brother, that I made a covenant with these false sons of Troy. Right well, indeed, I know that oath and sacrifice are not in vain. For though Zeus fulfil not now his purpose, yet will he take vengeance at the last, and the guilty shall suffer, they and their wives, and their children. Troy shall fall; but woe is me if thou shouldst die, Menelaüs.

For the Greeks will straight go back to their fatherland, and the fair Helen will be left a boast to the sons of Troy, and I shall have great shame when one of them shall say, as he leaps on the tomb of the brave Menelaüs, 'Surely the great Agamemnon has avenged himself well; for he brought an army hither, but now is gone back to his home, but left Menelaüs here.' May the earth swallow me up before that day!"

"Nay," said Menelaüs; "fear not, for the arrow hath but grazed the skin."

Then King Agamemnon bade fetch the physician. So the herald fetched Machaon, the physician. And Machaon came, and drew forth the arrow, and when he had wiped away the blood he put healing drugs upon the wound, which Cheiron, the wise healer, had given to his father.

But while this was doing, King Agamemnon went throughout the host, and if he saw any one stirring himself to get ready for the battle he praised him and gave him good encouragement; but whomsoever he saw halting and lingering and slothful, him he blamed and rebuked whether he were common man or chief. The last that he came to was Diomed, son of Tydeus with Sthenelus, son of Capaneus, standing by his side. And Agamemnon spake: "How is this, son of Tydeus? Shrinkest thou from the battle? This was not thy father's wont. I never saw him, indeed, but I have heard that he was braver than all other men. Once he came to Mycenæ with great Polyneices to gather allies against Thebes. And the men of Mycenæ would have sent them, only Zeus showed evil signs from heaven and forbade them. Then the Greeks sent Tydeus on an embassy to Thebes, where he found many of the sons of Cadmus feasting in the palace of Eteocles; but Tydeus was not afraid, though he was but one among many. He challenged them to contend with him in sport, and in everything he prevailed. But the sons of Cadmus bare it ill, and they laid an ambush for Tydeus as he went back, fifty men with two leaders, Mæon and Lycophon. But Tydeus slew them all, leaving only Mæon alive, that he might carry back the tidings to Thebes. Such was thy father; but his son is worse in battle, but better, it may be, in speech."

Nothing said Diomed, for he reverenced the King; but Sthenelus cried out: "Why speakest thou false, King Agamemnon, knowing the truth? We are not worse but better than our fathers. Did not we take Thebes, though we had fewer men than they, who indeed took it not?" But Diomed frowned and said: "Be silent, friend. I blame not King Agamemnon, that he rouses the Greeks to battle. Great glory will it be to him if they take the city, and great loss if they be worsted. But it is for us to be valiant."

So he passed through all the host. And the Greeks went forward to the battle, as the waves that curl themselves, then dash upon the shore, throwing high the foam. In order they went after their chiefs; you had thought them dumb, so silent were they. But the Trojans were like a flock of ewes which wait to be milked, and bleat hearing the voice of their lambs, so confused a cry went out from their army, for there were men of many tongues gathered together. And on either side the gods urged them on.

Among the Trojan ranks was Ares, and among the Greeks Athené, and with her Fear, and Flight, and Strife that never grows weary, sister and comrade of Ares. Mean is her stature at the first, but in the end she holds her head to heaven, while she walks with her feet upon the earth.

# CHAPTER VI.

### THE VALIANT DEEDS OF DIOMED.

WHEN the armies were come into one place, they dashed together with buckler and spear; and there was a great crash of shields that met, boss upon boss. Next rose up a great moaning of them that were stricken down, and shouting of the conquerors; and the ground ran with blood. As when two torrents, swollen with rains of winter, join their waters in a hollow ravine at the meeting of the glens, and the shepherds hear the din far off among the hills, even so, with a mighty noise and great confusion, did the two armies meet.

Antilochus, son of Nestor, was the first to slay a man of Troy, Ecepholus by name, smiting him through the helmet on the forehead. Like a tower he fell, and Elphenor the Eubœan sought to drag him away, that he might strip him of his arms. But Agenor smote him with his spear as he stooped, so baring his side to a wound. Dreadful was the fight around his body. Like wolves the Trojans and the Greeks rushed upon each other. And Ajax Telamon slew Simœisius (so they called him, because he was born on the banks of Simois). He fell as a poplar falls, and Antiphon, son of King Priam, aimed at Ajax, but, missing him, slew Leucus, the valiant comrade of Ulysses. And Ulysses, in great anger, stalked through the foremost fighters, brandishing his spear, and the sons of Troy gave way, and when he hurled it he slew Democoön, a son of Priam. Then Hector and the foremost ranks of Troy were borne backward, till Apollo cried from the heights of Pergamos: "On, Trojans! The flesh of these Greeks is not stone or iron, that ye cannot pierce it. Know, too, that the mighty Achilles does not fight to-day." But on the other side Athené urged on the Greeks to battle. Then Peiros the Thracian slew Diores, first striking him to the ground with a huge stone, and then piercing him with his spear; and him in turn Thoas of Ætolia slew, but could not spoil of his arms, so strongly did the men of Thrace defend the body. Then

Athené roused Diomed to battle, making a fire shine from his helmet, bright as Orion shines in the vintage time. First there met him two warriors, sons of Dares, priest of Hephæstus, Phegeus and Idæus, the one fighting on foot and the other from his chariot. First Phegeus threw his spear and missed his aim; but Diomed missed not, smiting him through the breast. And Idæus, when he saw his brother fall, fled, Hephæstus saving him, lest the old man should be altogether bereaved. And when the Trojans saw that of the two sons of Dares one had perished and the other had fled, their hearts were troubled within them.

Then did Athené take Ares by the hand, and say to him: "Come, let us leave the Greeks and the men of Troy to fight, and let Zeus give the glory to whom he will; only let us draw back, and avoid his wrath."

So she drew back fierce Ares from the war, and caused him to sit by the banks of Scamander. Then did the Greeks beat back the men of Troy. And each of the chiefs slew a foe; but there was none like Diomed, who raged through the battle so furiously that you could not tell with which host he was, whether with the Greeks or-with the sons of Troy. Then Pandarus aimed an arrow at him, and smote him in the right shoulder as he was rushing forward, and cried aloud: "On, great-hearted sons of Troy, the bravest of the Greeks is wounded! Soon, methinks, will his strength fail him, unless Apollo has deceived me."

So he spake exulting, but the arrow quelled not Diomed. Only he leapt down from the chariot, and spake to Sthenelus, his charioteer, "Come down, and draw this arrow from my shoulder." Then Sthenelus drew it, and the blood spirted out from the wound. And Diomed prayed to Athené: "O Goddess, if ever thou didst love my father, and stand beside him in the fiery war, be thou a friend to me also; let me come within a spear's cast of this man who hath wounded me, and who boasteth himself over me, saying that I shall not long look upon the shining of the sun."

So he prayed, and Athené heard; and she made light his hands and his feet, and stood beside him, and spake: " Be bold now, O

Diomed, and fight with the men of Troy!
I have breathed into thy heart the spirit that
was in Tydeus, thy father, and I have taken
away the mist that was upon thine eyes, that
thou mayest know god from man. Fight not
thou with any of the immortals, if a god should
come in thy way; only if Aphrodité comes
into the battle, her thou mayest wound."

So spake Athené, and went her way; and
Diomed turned back to the battle, and mingled
with the foremost. Eager he had been before
to fight, but now his eagerness was increased
threefold. Even as a lion whom a shepherd
wounds a little as he leaps into the fold, but
kills not, and the man escapes into his house,
and the sheep flee in their terror, falling hud-
dled in a heap, even so did Diomed rage
among the men of Troy.

Many did he slay, as the two sons of Eury-
damas, the old dreamer of dreams, who read
no dream to them aright of safe return, and
the two sons of Phœnops, darlings of their
father, for they were his only sons, and he had
none besides, and two sons of Priam, riding in
one chariot. As a lion leaps into the herd,

and breaks the neck of a heifer or a cow, even so did Diomed dash them struggling from the chariot, and gave their horses to his followers, that they should drive them to the ships.

Æneas saw him, and thought how he might stay him in his course. So he passed through the host till he found Pandarus. "Pandarus," he said, "where are thy bow and arrows? See how this man deals death through the ranks. Send a shaft at him, first making thy prayer to Zeus."

Then Pandarus answered: "This man, methinks, is Diomed. The shield and the helmet and the horses are his. And yet I know not whether he is not a god. Some god, at least, stands by him and guards him. But now I sent an arrow at him, and smote him on the shoulder, right through the corselet, and thought that I had slain him; but lo! I have harmed him not at all. And now I know not what to do, for here I have no chariot. Eleven, indeed, there are at home, in the house of my father Lycaon, and the old man was earnest with me that I should bring one of them; but I would not, fearing for my horses, lest they should not have provender enough. So I came, trusting in my bow, and lo! it has failed me these two times. Two of the chiefs I have hit, Menelaüs and Diomed, and from each have seen the red blood flow, yet have I not harmed them. Surely, if ever I return safe to my home, I will break this useless bow."

"Nay," said Æneas, "talk not thus. Climb into my chariot, and see what horses we have in Troy. They will carry us safe to the city, even should Diomed prevail against us. But take the rein and the whip, and I will fight; or, if thou wilt, fight thou, and I will drive."

"Nay," said Pandarus, "let the horses have the driver whom they know. It might lose us both, should we turn to flee, and they linger or start aside, missing their master's voice."

So Pandarus mounted the chariot, and they drove together against Diomed. And Sthenelus saw them coming, and said to his comrades: "I see two mighty warriors, Lycaon and Æneas. It would be well that we should go back to our chariot."

But Diomed frowned, and said: "Talk not

of going back. Thou wilt talk in vain to me. As for my chariot, I care not for it. As I am will I go against these men. Both shall not return safe, even if one should escape. But do thou stay my chariot where it is, tying the reins to the rail; and if I slay these men, mount the chariot of Æneas and drive it into the host of the Greeks. There are no horses under the sun such as these, for they are of the breed which Zeus himself gave to King Tros."

Meanwhile Pandarus and Æneas were coming near, and Pandarus cast his spear. Right through the shield of Diomed it passed, and reached the corselet, and Pandarus cried:—

"Thou art hit in the loin. This, methinks, will lay thee low."

"Nay," said Diomed, "thou hast missed and not hit at all."

And as he spake he threw his spear. Through nose and teeth and tongue it passed, and stood out below the chin. Headlong from the chariot he fell, and his armour clashed about him. Straightway Æneas leapt off with spear and shield to guard the body of his friend, and stood as a lion stands over a carcass. But Diomed lifted a great stone, such as two men of our day could scarcely carry, and cast it. It struck Æneas on the hip, crushing the bone. The hero stooped on his knee, clutching the ground with his hand, and darkness covered his eyes. That hour he had perished, but his mother Aphrodité caught him in her white arms, and threw her veil about him. But even so, Diomed was loath to let his foe escape, and knowing that the goddess was not of those who mingle in the battle, he rushed on her and wounded her on the wrist, and the blood gushed out — such blood (they call it *ichor*) as flows in the veins of the immortal gods, who eat not the meat and drink not the drink of men. With a loud shriek she dropped her son, but Apollo caught him up and covered him with a dark mist, lest perchance one of the Greeks should spy him and slay him.

But Diomed called aloud after Aphrodité: " Haste thee from the battle, daughter of Zeus. It is enough for thee to beguile weak women."

Wildly did the goddess rush from the battle.

And Iris, swift as the winds, took her by the hand, and led her out of the press, for she was tormented with the pain. She found Ares on the left of the field, and knelt before him, begging for his horses with many prayers. " Help me, dear brother," she said, " and lend me thy horses to carry me to Olympus, for I am tormented with a wound which a mortal man gave me, even Diomed, who would fight with Father Zeus himself."

Then Ares gave her his chariot, and Iris took the reins, and touched the horses with the whip. Speedily came they to Olympus, and then Iris reined in the horses, and Aphrodité fell on the lap of her mother Dioné, who took her daughter in her arms, and caressed her, . saying: —

" Dear child, which of the immortals hath harmed thee thus?"

Aphrodité answered, " No immortal hath done it, but a mortal man, even Diomed, who now fighteth with the immortal gods."

But Dioné answered: " Bear up and endure thy pain, for many who dwell in Olympus have suffered pain at the hands of mortal men. So

Ares endured when the two giants bound him with mighty bonds. Nineteen months he lay in a jar of bronze, aye, and had perished there, but that Hermes stole him therefrom. Pain also did Hera endure when the strong Hercules smote her in the breast with a three-pointed arrow; and Pluto also when the same man struck him at Pylos, where are the gates of hell. And now Athené hath urged on the son of Tydeus. Fool that he is! he knoweth not that brief are the days of him who would fight with the immortal gods. No children shall stand at his knee and call him father. Let him take heed, for all that he is so strong!"

So spake she, and wiped the moisture from the wound with both her hands, and the grievous hurt was healed. But Hera and Athené looked on and mocked. And Athené said to Zeus, "Now hath thy daughter been moving one of the Greek women to follow the Trojans whom she loveth so well, and lo! she hath wounded her hand with the pin of a golden brooch."

But the father smiled, and called Aphrodité

to him, and said, " My child, deeds of war are not for thee, but love and marriage ; leave the rest to Athené and Ares."

Meanwhile Diomed sprang upon Æneas, though he knew that Apollo himself held him. He regarded not the god, for he was eager to slay the hero and to strip off his arms. Thrice he sprang, and thrice Apollo dashed back his shining shield. The fourth time Apollo warned him with awful words, " Beware, son of Tydeus, and fall back, nor think to match thyself with gods." But Apollo carried Æneas out of the battle, and laid him down in his own temple in the citadel of Troy, and there Artemis and Latona healed him of his wound. And all the while the Trojans and the Greeks were fighting, as they thought, about his body, for Apollo had made a likeness of the hero and thrown it down in their midst. Then Sarpedon the Lycian spake to Hector with bitter words : —

" Where are thy boasts, Hector ? Thou saidst that thou couldst guard thy city, without thy people or thy allies, thou alone, with thy brothers and thy brothers-in-law. But I cannot see even one of them. They go and hide themselves, as dogs before a lion. It is we, your allies, who maintain the battle. I have come from far to help thy people, — from Lycia, where I left wife and child and wealth, — nor do I shrink from the fight, but thou shouldst do thy part."

And the words stung Hector to the heart. He leapt from his chariot and went through the host, urging them to the battle. And on the other side the Greeks strengthened themselves. But Ares brought back Æneas whole from his wound, and gave him courage and might. Right glad were his comrades to see him, nor did they ask him any question; scant leisure was there for questions that day. Then were done many valiant deeds, nor did any bear himself more bravely than Æneas. Two chieftains of the Greeks he slew, Crethon and Orsilochus, who came from the banks of Alpheüs. Sore vexed was Menelaüs to see them fall, and he rushed to avenge them, Ares urging him on, for he hoped that Æneas would slay him. But Antilochus, Nestor's son, saw him go, and hasted to his side that he might help him.  So they went and slew Pylæmenes, King of the Paphlagonians, and Medon, his charioteer.  Then Hector rushed to the front, and Ares was by his side.  Diomed saw him, and the god also, for his eyes were opened that day, and he fell back a space and cried : —

"O my friends! here Hector comes; nor is he alone, but Ares is with him in the shape of a mortal man.  Let us give place, still keeping our faces to the foe, for men must not fight with gods."

Then drew near to each other Sarpedon the Lycian and Tlepolemus, the son of Hercules, the one a son and the other a grandson of Zeus.  First Tlepolemus spake : —

"What art thou doing here, Sarpedon?  Surely 'tis a false report that thou art a son of Zeus.  The sons of Zeus in the old days were better men than thou art, such as my Father Hercules, who came to this city when Laomedon would not give him the horses which he had promised, and brake down the walls and wasted the streets.  No help, methinks, wilt thou be to the sons of Troy, slain here by my hands."

But Sarpedon answered: "He, indeed, spoiled Troy, for Laomedon did him grievous wrong. But thou shalt not fare so, but rather meet with thy death."

Then they both hurled their spears, aiming truly, both of them. For Sarpedon smote Tlepolemus in the neck, piercing it through so that he fell dead, and Tlepolemus smote Sarpedon in the left thigh, driving the spear close to the bone, but slaying him not, for his Father Zeus warded off the doom of death. And his comrades carried him out of the battle, sorely burdened with the spear, which no one had thought to take out of the wound. And as he was borne along, Hector passed by, and Sarpedon rejoiced to see him, and cried:—

" Son of Priam, suffer me not to become a prey to the Greeks; let me at least die in your city; for Lycia I may see no more, nor wife, nor child."

But Hector heeded him not, so eager was he for the battle. So his comrades carried him to the great beech tree and laid him down, and one of them drew the spear out of his thigh.

When it was drawn out he fainted, but the cool north wind blew and revived him, and he breathed again.

But all the while Hector, with Ares at his side, dealt death and destruction through the ranks of the Greeks. Hera and Athené saw him where they sat on the top of Olympus, and were wroth. So they went to Father Zeus, and prayed that it might be lawful to them to stop him in his fury. And Zeus said, " Be it as you will." So they yoked the horses to the chariot of Hera and passed down to earth, the horses flying at every stride over so much space as a man sees who sits upon a cliff and looks across the sea to where it meets the sky. They alighted on the spot where the two rivers Simoïs and Scamander join their streams. There they loosed the horses from the yoke, and then sped like doves to where the bravest of the Greeks stood round King Diomed. There Hera took the shape of Stentor with the lungs of bronze, whose voice was as the voice of fifty men, and cried: " Shame, men of Greece! When Achilles went to the battle, the men of Troy came not beyond the gates, but now they fight far from the city, even by the ships." But Athené went to Diomed, where he stood wiping away the blood from the wound where Pandarus had struck him with the arrow. And she spake: "Surely the son of Tydeus is little like to his sire. Small of stature was he, but a keen fighter. But thou — whether it be weariness or fear that keeps thee back I know not — canst scarcely be a true son of Tydeus."

But Diomed answered: " Nay, great goddess, for I know thee who thou art, daughter of Zeus, it is not weariness or fear that keeps me back. 'Tis thy own command that I heed. Thou didst bid me fight with none other of the immortal gods but only with Aprodité, should she come to the battle. Therefore I give place, for I see Ares lording it through the ranks of war."

Then Athené spake: " Heed not Ares; drive thy chariot at him, and smite him with the spear. This very morning he promised that he would help the Greeks, and now he hath changed his purpose."

And as she spake she pushed Sthenelus,

DIOMED CASTING HIS SPEAR AGAINST ARES.

who drove the chariot, so that he leapt out upon the ground, and she mounted herself and caught the reins and lashed the horses. So the two went together, and they found Ares where he had just slain Periphas the Ætolian. But Athené had donned the helmet of Hades, which whosoever puts on straightway becomes invisible, for she would not that Ares should see her who she was. The god saw Diomed come near, and left Periphas, and cast his spear over the yoke of the chariot, eager to slay the hero. But Athené caught the spear in her hand, and turned it aside, so that it flew vainly through the air. Then Diomed in turn thrust forward his spear, and Athené leant upon it, so that it pierced the loin of Ares, where his girdle was clasped. And Ares shouted with the pain, loud as a host of men, thousands nine or ten, shouts when it joins in battle. And the Greeks and Trojans trembled as they heard. And Diomed saw the god go up to Olympus as a thunder-cloud goes up when the wind of the south blows hot.

By the side of Zeus did he sit down, and

showed the immortal blood as it flowed from the wound, and cried: "Father Zeus, canst thou contain thyself, seeing such deeds as these? See now this daughter of thine, how she is bent on evil and mischief. All we that dwell in Olympus are obedient to thee; but her thou checkest not with word or deed; she is thy child, forsooth, a very child of mischief. And now she hath set on this bold Diomed to wreak his madness on the immortal gods: first he wounded Aphrodité on the wrist; then he rushed on me; my swift feet bare me away, else surely I had suffered the pains of death among the carcasses of the slain."

But Zeus frowned on him, and spake: "Come not to me with thy complaints, for of all the Olympian gods thou vexest me the most, for battle and strife are ever dear to thee. 'Tis thy mother Hera that hath put thee to this pain. Yet I may not suffer thee to endure the anguish any more, for thou art my child; verily, hadst thou been the offspring of any other god, thou hadst lain long since deep down in Tartarus below the giant race."

Then Zeus called Pæon the healer, and bade

him tend the wound; and he, sprinkling on it pain-dispelling simples, cured it of its smart. Then Hebe gave to Ares the bath, and clad him in fair array, and he sat down by Zeus, rejoicing.

# CHAPTER VII.

## GLAUCUS AND DIOMED.

Now when Ares had departed, the Greeks prevailed again, slaying many of the sons of Troy and of their allies. But at last Helenus, the wise seer, spake to Hector and Æneas:—

"Cause the army to draw back to the walls, and go through the ranks and give them such strength and courage as ye may. And do thou, Hector, when thou hast so done, pass into the city, and bid thy mother go with the daughters of Troy, and take the costliest robe that she hath, and lay it on the knees of Athené in her temple, vowing therewith to sacrifice twelve heifers, if perchance she may have pity upon us, and keep this Diomed from our walls. Surely there is no Greek so strong as he; we did not fear even Achilles' self so much as we fear this man to-day, so dreadful is he and fierce. Go, and we will make such stand meanwhile as we can."

Then Hector passed through the ranks, bidding them be of good heart, and so departed to the city.

And when he was gone, Glaucus the Lycian and Diomed met in the space between the two hosts. Then first spake Diomed: " Tell me, thou mighty man of valour, who thou art of mortal men, for never before have I seen thee in the battle; but now thou comest out far before the ranks of thy fellows, and art willing to abide my spear. Luckless are the fathers of them that set themselves against my might. Yet, if thou be one of the immortal gods, and hast come down from heaven, I fight thee not. I dare not match myself with the gods of heaven. For King Lycurgus, son of Dryas, that fought with the gods, lived not long. Through the land of Nysa did he drive the nursing mothers of Bacchus, wielding an ox-goad in his fury, so that they dropped their wands for fear; and Bacchus also fled and leapt into the waves of the salt sea, being sore afraid; and Thetis took him to her bosom. Nevertheless, the gods that live at ease were wroth with Lycurgus, for all that he thus prevailed, and Zeus took from him the sight of his eyes; nor did he live many days, seeing that he was abhorred of all the gods. Therefore, I will not fight against any god; but if thou art mortal man, such as eat of the fruits of the field, come thou near, that I may give thee to death."

To him Glaucus the Lycian made answer: "Valiant son of Tydeus, why seekest thou to know my name and lineage, and the generations of my fathers? For the generations of men are as of the leaves of the wood. The wind scattereth them on the ground, and the wood bringeth forth others in the springtime. So is it with the generations of men — one goeth, and another cometh. Yet, if thou wilt know these things, hearken unto me. There is in the midst of Argos a certain city, Ephyre, wherein dwelt Sisyphus, son of Æolus, that was the craftiest of men. This Sisyphus begat Glaucus, and Glaucus begat Bellerophon, whom the gods made beautiful and strong above all other men. But Prœtus, who, by the ordering of Zeus, bare rule over the land of Argos, hated him, and drave him forth from among the people. And the cause was this: fair Anteia, that was wife to the King, loved Bellerophon; but he would not hearken to her words; for he was wise and upright of heart. Then Anteia spake falsely to the King, her husband, saying, 'If thou wouldst not die, O King, thou must slay this Bellerophon, for he would have had me love him, only I said him nay.' So she spake, and the King was very wroth when he heard her saying. He slew not Bellerophon, for shame forbade him; but he sent him to Lycia, to the King, the father of Anteia, and with him he sent a token of death, folding it in a tablet, that he might show it to the King and the King might slay him. So Bellerophon journeyed to Lycia, and the gods kept him safely on the way. And when he was come to the land, even to the river of Xanthus, then the King of the country made a great entertainment for him. Nine days he feasted him, slaying on every day an ox. And when the morning of the tenth day was come, he inquired of him his errand, and would see what writing he had brought. And when he had noted the token of death, he sent Bellerophon to slay the beast which no man could conquer, even the Chimæra. Now this Chimæra was of the race of the gods and not of the race of men. Her face was the face of a lion, and her hinder parts were the tail of a serpent, and her middle the shape of a goat, and the breath of her mouth was flaming fire. Her, indeed, he slew, for the gods guided him in his deed. And after this he fought with the Solymi, that were valiant men of war; and never, he was wont to say in aftertime, did he encounter warriors so fierce and strong as they. Then, again, he fought with the Amazons, that were women with the strength of men, and prevailed over them. But when he was coming back from these doings, the King devised against him a crafty device. For he set an ambush against him, choosing for it the bravest men of all the land of Lycia. But not one man of these returned to his home, for Bellerophon slew them all. And when the King knew how valiant he was, and that he was of the race of the gods, he would keep him in the land, and gave him his daughter to his wife, yea, and with her the half of

his kingdom. The men of Lycia also meas-
ured out for him a fair domain of vineyards
and plough-land. And his wife bare to Bellerophon three children; but after this the wrath
of the gods came upon him, and he wandered
alone over the Aleian plain, devouring his
heart in sorrow, and avoiding the paths of
men. And of his children, Peisander, his
son, fell in battle, fighting against the Solymi,
and Laodamia died smitten by the arrow of
Artemis, after that she had borne a son to
Zeus, even Sarpedon. But he had yet another
son, by name Hippolochus. He is my father,
and he sent me to Troy, saying to me, 'Strive
evermore to be the first and to overpass other
men, and shame not the house of thy fathers,
who held high place in Ephyre and in the
broad land of Lycia.' This, then, noble Diomed, is the house and lineage of which I claim
to be."

So spake Glaucus, and Diomed was glad at
heart. His spear he drave into the earth, and
he spake pleasant words to the prince: " Verily, thou art by inheritance a friend of my
house. For long ago great Œneus entertained

Bellerophon in his dwelling, keeping him twenty days. Goodly gifts did they give one to the other. Œneus gave to Bellerophon a belt richly broidered with purple, and Bellerophon gave to Œneus a cup of gold with a mouth on either side. This I left when I came hither, in my palace at home. Now Œneus begat Tydeus, and Tydeus was my father. My father he was, but I remember him not; for he left me when I was a little child, and perished with the chiefs, his companions, fighting against Thebes. Therefore, I am thy friend and host when thou comest to the land of Argos, and thou art mine if any chance shall bring me to Lycia. But now, let each of us shun the spear of the other, yea, in the closest press of the battle. Many sons of Troy there are, and many of their brave allies, whom I may slay if the gods deliver them into my hands, and my feet be swift to overtake them. And thou also hast many Greeks to slay if thou canst. But now let us make exchange of arms and armour, that both the Greeks and the men of Troy may know that we are friends by inheritance."

So spake Tydeus. And the two chiefs leapt down from their chariots, and clasped each the hand of the other, and pledged their faith. Then Zeus changed the wisdom of Glaucus to folly, so that he gave his armour in exchange for the armour of Diomed, gold for bronze, the price of five-score oxen for the price of nine.

## CHAPTER VIII.

### HECTOR AND ANDROMACHÉ.

HECTOR came into the city by the Scæan gates, and as he went wives and mothers crowded about him, asking how it had fared with their husbands and sons. But he said nought, save to bid them pray; and indeed there was sore news for many, if he had told that which he knew. Then he came to the palace of King Priam, and there he saw Hecuba, his mother, and with her Laodicé, fairest of her daughters. She caught him by the hand and said:—

"Why hast thou come from the battle, my son? Do the Greeks press thee hard, and art thou minded to pray to Father Zeus from the citadel? Let me bring thee honey-sweet wine, that thou mayest pour out before him, aye, and that thou mayest drink thyself, and gladden thy heart."

But Hector said: "Give me not wine, my

mother, lest thou weaken my knees and make me forget my courage. Nor must I pour out an offering with Zeus thus, with unwashed hands. But do thou gather the mothers of Troy together, and go to the temple of Athené and take a robe, the one that is the most precious and beautiful in thy stores, and lay it on the knees of the goddess, and pray her to keep this dreadful Diomed from the walls of Troy; and forget not to vow therewith twelve heifers as a sacrifice. As for me, I will go and seek Paris, if perchance he will come with me to the war. Would that the earth might open and swallow him up, for of a truth he is a curse to King Priam and to Troy."

Then went Queen Hecuba into her house, and gave command to her maids that they should assemble the aged women of the city. Afterwards she went to her store-chamber, where lay the well-wrought robes, work of Sidonian women, which Paris himself brought from Sidon, when he sailed upon the broad sea. bringing home with him high-born Helen. The fairest robe of all did the Queen take. Bright as a star it was, and it lay the undermost of all.

And when she and the aged women that were with her came to the temple of Athené that was in the citadel, Theano, Antenor's wife, whom the Trojans had made priestess of Athené, opened the doors to them. They lifted their hands, and cried aloud, and Theano laid the garment on the knees of the goddess, and spake, saying: —

"Lady Athené, that keepest the city, break now the spear of Diomed, and let him fall upon his face before the Scæan gates. So will we sacrifice to thee twelve heifers that have not felt the goad, if only thou wilt have pity upon our town, and on the wives and little ones of the men of Troy."

So prayed Theano, but Athené heeded not her words.

Meanwhile Hector went to the house of Paris, where it stood on the citadel, near to his own dwelling and the dwelling of Priam. He found him busy with his arms, and the fair Helen sat near him and gave their tasks to her maidens.

When Hector saw his brother, he spake to him bitter words, taunting him, as if it were

Hector chiding Paris.

by reason of his anger that he stood aloof from the battle. " Verily thou doest not well to be angry. The people perish about the walls, and the war burns hot round the city; and all for thy sake. Rouse thee, lest it be consumed."

And Paris answered: " Brother, thou hast spoken well. It was not in wrath that I sat here. I was vexed at my sore defeat. But now my wife has urged me to join the battle; and truly it is well, for victory comes now to one and now to another. Wait thou, then, till I put on my arms, or, if thou wouldst depart, I will overtake thee."

Then spake Helen with soothing words: "O my brother, would that I had perished on the day when my mother bare me! But if this might not be, would that the gods had made me the wife of one who feared the blame of his fellow-men; but this man hath no understanding, no, nor ever will have. Surely, he shall eat of the fruit of his ill-doing. But come in, sit thee down in this chair, for my heart is weary because of my sin and of the sin of my husband. Verily Zeus hath ordained for us an evil fate, so that our story shall be sung in days that are yet to come."

But Hector said: "Ask me not to rest, for I am eager to help the men of Troy, for verily their need is sore. But do thou urge thy husband that he overtake me while I am yet within the city, for now I go to my home that I may see my wife and my little son, because I know not whether I shall return to them again."

So Hector departed and went to his own home, seeking his wife Andromaché, but found her not, for she was on a tower of the wall with her child and her child's nurse, weeping sore for fear. And Hector spake to the maids : —

"Tell me, whither went the white-armed Andromaché; to see some sister-in-law, or to the temple of Athené with the mothers of Troy?"

"Nay," said an aged woman, keeper of the house. "She went to one of the towers of the wall, for she had heard that the Greeks were pressing our people hard. She hasted like as she were mad, and the nurse carried the child."

So Hector ran through the city to the Scæan gates, and there Andromaché spied him, and hasted to meet him — Andromaché, daughter of King Eëtion, of Thebé-under-Placus. And with her was the nurse, bearing the young child on her bosom — Hector's only child, beautiful, headed as a star. His father called him Scamandrius, after the river, but the sons of Troy called him Astyanax, the " City-King," because it was his father who saved the city. Silently he smiled when he saw the child, but Andromaché clasped his hand and wept, and said : —

" O Hector, thy courage will bring thee to death. Thou hast no pity on thy wife and child, but sparest not thyself, and all the Greeks will rush on thee and slay thee. It were better for me, losing thee, to die; for I have no comfort but thee. My father is dead, for Achilles slew him in Thebé — slew him but spoiled him not, so much he reverenced him. With his arms he burnt him, and the mountain-nymphs planted poplars about his grave. Seven brethren I had, and they all fell in one day by the hand of the great Achilles.

And my mother, she is dead, for when she had been ransomed, Artemis smote her with an arrow in her father's house. But thou art father to me, and mother, and brother, and husband also. Have pity, then, and stay here upon the wall, lest thou leave me a widow and thy child an orphan. And set the people here in array by this fig tree, where the city is easiest to be taken; for there come the bravest of the Greeks, Ajax the Greater, and Ajax the Less, and Idomeneus, and the two sons of Atreus, and the son of Tydeus."

But Hector said: " Nay, let these things be my care. I would not that any son or daughter of Troy should see me skulking from the war. And my own heart loathes the thought, and bids me fight in the front. Well I know, indeed, that Priam, and the people of Priam, and holy Troy, will perish. Yet it is not for Troy, or for the people, or even for my father or my mother that I care so much, as for thee in the day when some Greek shall carry thee away captive, and thou shalt ply the loom or carry the pitcher in the land of Greece. And some one shall say when he sees thee, ' This was

THE MEETING OF HECTOR AND ANDROMACHE

Hector's wife, who was the bravest of the sons of Troy.' May the earth cover me before that day!"

Then Hector stretched out his arms to his child. But the child drew back into the bosom of his nurse, with a loud cry, fearing the shining bronze and the horse-hair plume which nodded awfully from his helmet top. Then father and mother laughed aloud. And Hector took the helmet from his head, and laid it on the ground, and caught his child in his hands, and kissed him and dandled him, praying aloud to Father Zeus and all the gods.

"Grant, Father Zeus and all ye gods, that this child may be as I am, great among the sons of Troy; and may they say some day, when they see him carrying home the bloody spoils from the war, 'A better man than his father, this,' and his mother shall be glad at heart."

Then he gave the child to his mother, and she clasped him to her breast, and smiled a tearful smile. And her husband's heart was moved; and he stroked her with his hand, and spake : —

" Be not troubled over much. No man shall slay me against the ordering of fate; but as for fate, that, methinks, no man may escape, be he coward or brave. But go, ply thy tasks, the shuttle and the loom, and give their tasks to thy maidens, and let men take thought for the battle."

Then Hector took up his helmet from the ground, and Andromaché went her way to her home, oft turning back her eyes. And when she was come, she and all her maidens wailed for the living Hector as though he were dead, for she thought that she should never see him any more returning safe from the battle.

And as Hector went his way, Paris came running, clad in shining arms, like to some proud steed which has been fed high in his stall, and now scours the plain with head aloft and mane streaming over his shoulders. And he spake to Hector: —

" I have kept thee, I fear, when thou wast in haste, nor came at thy bidding."

But Hector answered: " No man can blame thy courage, only thou wilfully heldest back from the battle. Therefore do the sons of Troy speak shame of thee. But now let us go to the war."

So they went together out of the gates, and fell upon the hosts of the Greeks and slew many chiefs of fame, and Glaucus the Lycian went with them.

# CHAPTER IX.

## THE DUEL OF HECTOR AND AJAX.

Now when Athené saw that the Greeks were perishing by the hand of Hector and his companions, it grieved her sore.  So she came down from the heights of Olympus, if haply she might help them.  And Apollo met her and said:—

"Art thou come, Athené, to help the Greeks whom thou lovest?  Well, let us stay the battle for this day; hereafter they shall fight till the doom of Troy be accomplished."

But Athené answered, "How shall we stay it?"

And Apollo said, "We will set on Hector to challenge the bravest of the Greeks to fight with him, man to man."

So they two put the matter into the mind of Helenus the seer.  Then Helenus went near to Hector, and spake, saying:—

"Listen to me, for I am thy brother.  Cause the rest of the sons of Troy and of the Greeks to sit down, and do thou challenge the bravest of the Greeks to fight with thee, man to man. And be sure thou shalt not fall in the battle, for the will of the immortal gods is so."

Then Hector greatly rejoiced, and passed to the front of the army, holding his spear by the middle, and kept back the sons of Troy; and King Agamemnon did likewise with his own people. Then Hector spake: —

"Hear me, sons of Troy, and ye men of Greece. The covenant that we made one with another hath been broken, for Zeus would have it so, purposing evil to both, till either you shall take our high-walled city or we shall conquer you by your ships. But let one of you, who call yourselves champions of the Greeks, come forth and fight with me, man to man. And let it be so that if he vanquish me he shall spoil me of my arms, but give my body to my people, that they may burn it with fire; and if I vanquish him, I will spoil him of his arms, but give his body to the Greeks, that they may bury him and raise a great mound above him by the broad salt river of Hellespont. And so men of after days shall see it, sailing by, and say, 'This is the tomb of the bravest of the Greeks, whom Hector slew.' So shall my name live forever."

But all the Greeks kept silence, fearing to meet him in battle, but shamed to hold back. Then at last Menelaüs leapt forward and spake:—

"Surely now ye are women and not men. Foul shame it were should there be no man to stand up against this Hector. Lo! I will fight with him my own self, for the issues of battle are with the immortal gods."

So he spake in his rage rashly, courting death, for Hector was much stronger than he. Then King Agamemnon answered:—

"Nay, but this is folly, my brother. Seek not in thy anger to fight with one that is stronger than thou; for as for this Hector, even Achilles was loth to meet him. Sit thou down among thy comrades, and the Greeks will find some champion who shall fight with him."

And Menelaüs hearkened to his brother's words, and sat down. Then Nestor rose in the midst and spake:—

"Woe is me to-day for Greece! How would

the old Peleus grieve to hear such a tale! Well
I remember how he rejoiced when I told him
of the house and lineage of all the chieftains
of the Greeks, and now he would hear that
they cower before Hector, and are sore afraid
when he calls them to the battle. Surely he
would pray this day that he might die! Oh,
that I were such as I was in the old days,
when the men of Pylos fought with the Arcadians by the stream of Iardanus! Now the
leader of the Arcadians was Ereuthalion, and
he wore the arms of Areïthous, whom men
called 'Areïthous of the club,' because he fought
not with bow or spear, but with a club of iron.
Him Lycurgus slew, not by might, but by craft,
taking him in a narrow place where his club
of iron availed him not, and smiting him with
his spear. He slew him, and took his arms.
And when Lycurgus grew old he gave the
arms to Ereuthalion to wear. So Ereuthalion
wore them, and challenged the men of Pylos
to fight with him. But they feared him. Only
I, who was the youngest of all, stood forth,
and Athené gave me glory that day, for I slew
him, though he was the strongest and tallest

among the sons of men. Would that I were such to-day! Right soon would I meet this mighty Hector."

Then rose up nine chiefs of fame. First of all, King Agamemnon, lord of many nations, and next to him Diomed, son of Tydeus, and Ajax the Greater, and Ajax the Less, and then Idomeneus, and Meriones, who was his companion in arms, and Eurypylus, and Thoas, son of Andræmon, and the wise Ulysses.

Then Nestor said, " Let us cast lots who shall do battle with the mighty Hector."

So they threw the lots into the helmet of King Agamemnon, — a lot for each. And the people prayed, "Grant, ye gods, that the lot of Ajax the Greater may leap forth, or the lot of Diomed, or the lot of King Agamemnon." Then Nestor shook the lots in the helmet, and the one which they most wished leapt forth. For the herald took it through the ranks and showed it to the chiefs, but none knew it for his own till he came to where Ajax the Greater stood among his comrades. But Ajax had marked it with his mark, and put forth his hand for it, and claimed it, right glad at heart.

On the ground by his feet he threw it, and said : —

" Mine is the lot, my friends, and right glad I am, for I think that I shall prevail over the mighty Hector. But come, let me put on my arms ; and pray ye to Zeus, but silently, lest the Trojans hear, or aloud, if ye will, for no fear have we. Not by force or craft shall any one vanquish me, for not such are the men whom Salamis breeds."

So he armed himself and moved forwards, dreadful as Ares, smiling with grim face. With mighty strides he came, brandishing his long-shafted spear. And all the Greeks were glad to behold him, but the knees of the Trojans were loosened with fear, and great Hector's heart beat fast ; but he trembled not, nor gave place, seeing that he had himself called him to battle. So Ajax came near, holding before the great shield, like a wall, which Tychius, best of craftsmen, had made for him. Seven folds of bull's hide it had, and an eighth of bronze. Threateningly he spake : —

" Now shalt thou know, Hector, what manner of men there are yet among our chiefs, though

Achilles the lion-hearted is far away, sitting idly in his tent, in great wrath with King Agamemnon.  Do thou, then, begin the battle."

"Speak not to me, Zeus-descended Ajax," said Hector, "as though I were a woman or a child, knowing nothing of war.  Well I know all the arts of battle, to ply my shield this way and that, to guide my car through the tumult of steeds, and to stand fighting hand to hand.  But I would not smite so stout a foe by stealth, but openly, if it so befall."

And as he spake he hurled his long-shafted spear, and smote the great shield on the rim of the eighth fold, that was of bronze.  Through six folds it passed, but in the seventh it was stayed.  Then Ajax hurled his spear, striking Hector's shield.  Through shield it passed and corselet, and cut the tunic close against the loin; but Hector shrank away and escaped the doom of death.  Then, each with a fresh spear, they rushed together like lions or wild boars of the wood.  First Hector smote the middle of the shield of Ajax, but pierced it not, for the spear-point was bent back; then Ajax, with a great bound, drove his spear at Hector's shield and pierced it, forcing him back, and grazing his neck so that the black blood welled out. Yet did not Hector cease from the combat. A great stone and rough he caught up from the ground, and hurled it at the boss of the seven-fold shield. Loud rang the bronze, but the shield brake not. Then Ajax took a stone heavier by far, and threw it with all his might. It brake the shield of Hector, and bore him backwards, so that he fell at length with his shield above him. But Apollo raised him up. Then did both draw their swords; but ere they could join in close battle came the heralds, and held their sceptres between them, and Idæus, the herald of Troy, spake: —

"Fight no more, my sons; Zeus loves you both, and ye are both mighty warriors. That we all know right well. But now the night bids you cease, and it is well to heed its bidding."

Then said Ajax: "Nay, Idæus, but it is for Hector to speak, for he called the bravest of the Greeks to battle. And as he wills it, so will I."

And Hector said: "O Ajax, the gods have given thee stature and strength and skill, nor is there any better warrior among the Greeks. Let us cease then from the battle; we may yet meet again, till the gods give the victory to me or thee.  And now let us give gifts the one to the other, so that Trojans and Greeks may say, ' Hector and Ajax met in fierce fight and parted in friendship.'"

So Hector gave to Ajax a silver-studded sword with the scabbard and the sword-belt, and Ajax gave to Hector a buckler splendid with purple.  So they parted.  Right glad were the sons of Troy when they saw Hector returning safe.  Glad also were the Greeks, as they led Ajax rejoicing in his victory to King Agamemnon.  Whereupon the King called the chiefs to banquet together, and bade slay an ox of five years old, and Ajax he honoured most of all, giving him the chine.  And when the feast was ended, Nestor said: —

" It were well that we should cease awhile from war and burn the dead, for many, in truth, are fallen.  And we will build a great wall and dig a trench about it, and we will

HECTOR AND AJAX SEPARATED BY THE HERALDS.

make gates, wide that a chariot may pass through, so that our ships may be safe, if the sons of Troy should press us hard."

But the next morning came a herald from Troy to the chiefs, as they sat in council by the ship of King Agamemnon, and said : —

" This is the word of Priam and the men of Troy: Paris will give back all the treasures of the fair Helen, and many more besides ; but the fair Helen herself he will not give. But if this please you not, grant us a truce, that we may bury our dead."

Then Diomed spake, " Nay, we will not take the fair Helen's self, for a man may know, even though he be a fool, that the doom of Troy is come."

And King Agamemnon said, " Herald, thou hast heard the word of the Greeks, but as for the truce, be it as you will."

So the next day they burnt their dead, and the Greeks made a wall with gates and dug a trench about it. And when it was finished, even at sunset, they made ready a meal, and lo ! there came ships from Lemnos bringing wine, and Greeks bought thereof, some with bronze, and some with iron, and some with shields of ox hide. All night they feasted right joyously. The sons of Troy also feasted in their city. But the dreadful thunder rolled through the night, for Zeus was counselling evil against them.

# CHAPTER X.

### THE BATTLE ON THE PLAIN.

WHEN the next morning came Zeus called the gods to an assembly on the topmost ridge of Olympus, and spake to them, saying : —

"Hearken, gods and goddesses! Let none of you presume to go against my word. Whosoever of you shall succour either Greek or Trojan, him will I smite with the thunder, or else will cast him far down to the darkness of Tartarus, whose gates are iron and whose threshold bronze, and he shall know that I am chief among gods. And if ye will make trial of my strength, let down a chain of gold from heaven to earth, and take hold thereof, all ye gods and goddesses. Yet shall ye not drag down Zeus, no, though ye strive with all your might. But if I should draw with all my strength, I could lift you up, and earth and sea with you, and bind the chain about a horn of Olympus, and leave you hanging there. So much am I stronger than all besides."

Then all the gods sat silent and amazed. But at last spake Athené: " Surely we know, Father Zeus, that thy might brooks no control. Yet we have compassion of the Greeks, lest they should perish altogether. We will keep aloof from the war, according to thy command, but we will give them counsel."

And Zeus smiled upon her, and gave consent. Then he yoked to his chariot his swift horses, and touched them with his whip. Midway between heaven and earth they flew, and came to Ida, the mountain of many springs. There he stayed his course, and sat down amidst the peaks, looking on the city of Troy and the host of the Greeks.

The Greeks took their meal in haste, and armed themselves. The men of Troy also made them ready for battle in the city ; fewer they were in number than their foes, but not less eager for the fight, for indeed a sore need was upon them, the need to fight for children and wife. Then the gates were opened, and the people went quickly forth.

And the two hosts came together, buckler against buckler, and spear against spear, and the bosses of the shields clashed with a great ringing sound. While the day was increasing, neither this side prevailed nor that; but at noon Father Zeus stretched on high his golden scales, laying in them two weights of death; for the Greeks one, and one for the sons of Troy. By the middle he took the scales, and let them hang, and the scale of the Greeks sank lower. Then did he send his blazing bolt among the people from the heights of Ida, and they saw it and were dismayed.

Then could no man hold his ground. Only Nestor remained, and that against his will, for Paris had slain one of his chariot-horses with an arrow. And while the old man cut away the traces, came Hector through the press. Then had the old man perished, but Diomed was swift to mark. With a great cry he called Ulysses, and said : —

"Son of Laertes, whither dost thou flee, turning thy back like a coward in the press? See that no man thrust thee in the back with a spear. Tarry, rather, and keep back this fierce man of war from old Nestor."

So he spake, but Ulysses heeded not, fleeing fast to the ships.

Then rushed Diomed, alone as he was, into the foremost rank, and stood before the chariot of old Nestor, and spake: "Old sir, the younger fighters press thee sore; feeble thou art, and weak thy charioteer, and thy horses slow. Come, mount upon my chariot, and see what the horses of Tros can do, that I took from Æneas, — how they can flee, and follow and speed this way and that! To thy horses thy charioteer and mine shall look; come thou with me, and Hector shall see whether there is yet any strength in the spear of Diomed."

To this Nestor gave consent, and took the reins in his hand, and plied the whip. Soon they came near to Hector, and Diomed cast his spear. Hector he missed; but his charioteer, brave Eniopeus, he smote upon the breast, so that he fell from the chariot, and the swift horses started back. Hector's heart was dark with grief for his comrade; yet he let him lie where he fell, for he must needs find another charioteer.

Then there had been rout among the men of Troy, and they had been pent up in the city, as sheep in a fold, but that Zeus hurled a blazing thunderbolt. Right before the chariot of Diomed did it fall; and the horses crouched in fear, and Nestor let fall the reins from his hands, for he was sore afraid, and cried aloud: —

"Son of Tydeus, turn thy horses to flight; seest thou that Zeus is not with thee? To-day he giveth glory to Hector; to-morrow, haply, to thee. The purpose of Zeus none may hinder."

Then the son of Tydeus spake: "Old sir, thou sayest well; but this goeth to my heart, that Hector will say, 'Diomed fled before me, seeking the ships.' Then may the earth swallow me up!"

But Nestor made reply, "Though Hector call thee coward, yet will not the sons of Troy believe him, nor the daughters whose gallant husbands thou hast tumbled in the dust."

Then he turned his horses, and fled. But

Hector cried after him: "Art *thou* the man to whom the Greeks give high place in the feast, and plenteous cups of wine? Not so will they honour thee hereafter. Run, girl! run, coward! Shalt *thou* climb our walls, and carry away our daughters in thy ships?"

Then Diomed was very wroth, doubting whether to flee or to turn; but when he turned Zeus thundered from on high, making him afraid. And Hector bade the hosts of Troy be of good courage, for that Zeus was with them, and called to his horses: "Come, now, Bayard, and Whitefoot, and Flame of Fire, and Brilliant; forget not how the fair Andromaché has cared for you; aye, even before me, who am her husband. Carry me fast, that I may win old Nestor's shield, which men say is all of gold, and strip from the shoulders of Diomed the breastplate which Hephæstus wrought."

So the Greeks fled headlong within the wall which they had built, Hector driving them before him, and all the space between the wall and the ships was crowded with chariots and with men. Then verily had Hector burned the ships, had not Hera put it in the heart of King Agamemnon to exhort the Greeks to battle. On the ship of Ulysses, that was midmost of all, he stood, so that he could shout to either end, to where Ajax the Greater on one side, and Achilles on the other, had drawn up their ships. And he cried aloud: —

"Shame on you, ye Greeks! Where are now your boastings wherewith ye boasted in Lemnos, as ye ate the flesh of cattle, and drank from the brimming bowls of wine, how one man of you would outmatch five score, yea, ten score, of the sons of Troy? And now one single man is of more worth than you all! O Father Zeus, hast thou ever afflicted any king in such fashion? and yet have I never passed by altar of thine, but burnt on it the fat of beeves, praying that I might take the city of Troy. Grant us, now, that we may at least escape with our lives."

And Zeus hearkened to his prayer, and sent a sign from heaven, an eagle that held a kid in his claw; by the altar of Zeus, the god of warning, did he drop it, and the Greeks, when they saw it, took heart, and leaped upon the men of Troy, and rejoiced again in the battle.

Foremost of all was Diomed, who slew a Trojan, Agelaüs by name. Through the back he pierced him with his spear, driving it through his breast, and tumbled him from his chariot.

After him came the sons of Atreus, and either Ajax, and Idomeneus, and all the chiefs, and among them Teucer, who stood beneath the shield of Ajax Telamon, as he bent his bow. Ajax would lift his shield a little, and Teucer, peering out, would shoot a warrior in the throng. Then would he go back as a child to his mother, and Ajax would hide him beneath his shield. Eight warriors did he slay; and when Agamemnon saw him, he came near, and spake, saying: " Shoot on, Teucer, and be a light to thy people and to thy father Telamon. Surely when Zeus and Athené shall grant me the spoil of Troy, to thee, first after myself, will I give a goodly gift."

Teucer made reply: " Why dost thou urge me on that am myself so eager? Never have I ceased to ply them with mine arrows, according to my strength. Eight shafts have I launched, and every shaft has been buried in a warrior's flesh; but that man I cannot strike."

He spake, and shed another arrow from the string, aiming at Hector. Him he touched not, but he slew a son of Priam. Yet once again he shot, and slew this time the charioteer of Hector, striking him full upon the breast, as he rushed into battle. Then Hector's heart grew dark with rage and grief. He bade his brother Cebriones take the reins. Then he leapt from his chariot to the ground, and caught a stone in his hand, and went towards Teucer, desiring to crush him. Then Teucer took an arrow from the quiver and fitted it on the string, but as he drew the arrow to his shoulder, Hector smote him where the collar-bone stands between neck and breast, and snapped the bow-string, and numbed arm and wrist, so that the bow flew from his hand, and he fell upon his knee. But Ajax bestrode him, covering him with his shield, and two of his comrades bare him, groaning deeply, to the ships.

Then again did Zeus put courage into the hearts of the men of Troy, and they thrust the

Greeks back to the ditch; and Hector moved ever in the front, rejoicing in his strength. Even as a dog pursues a wild boar or a lion, and catches him by hip or thigh, so did Hector hang upon the Greeks, and smite the hindmost as they fled.

But Hera saw and pitied them, and spake to Athené: "Shall not thou and I have pity on the Greeks once again, if never more? Haply they will perish beneath the onslaught of Hector, who hath already wrought them manifold woe."

Athené made reply: "It is my father, who hath listened to Thetis, when she besought him to give honour to Achilles. But another day, may be, he will hearken unto me. Make ready, therefore, the horses, while I arm myself for the war. We will see whether Hector will be glad when he beholds thee and me in the forefront of the battle."

So Hera made ready the chariot, and Athené armed herself for the war. And when she was armed, Hera lashed the horses, and the great gates of heaven, where the Hours keep watch, opened before them.

But Zeus saw them from Ida, and said to Iris of the golden wings: " Go now, swift Iris, bid these two not come face to face with me, for our meeting would be ill for them. Verily I will hough their horses, and cast them from their chariot, and break the chariot in pieces. Not for ten years would they recover of their wounds should the lightning smite them."

So Iris hasted on her way, and gave the two goddesses the Father's message.

Then spake Hera to Athené: " No more do I counsel that we two should do battle with Zeus for the sake of mortal men. Let this one perish and that live, as it may befall, and Zeus dispense his judgments, as is meet and fit."

So they two went back to Olympus, and sat down in their chairs of gold, among the other gods, right heavy of heart.

Zeus also hastened from Ida to Olympus, and came into the assembly of the gods; but Hera and Athené sat apart, and spake not, and asked no question.

Then said Zeus: " Why are ye so cast down? Surely ye are not wearied with the war, with slaying the Trojans whom ye hate so sore. All the gods of Olympus may not overbear me ; and ye two tremble, or ever ye have looked on war."

He spake, and the two goddesses murmured where they sat side by side. Athené kept silence for all her wrath; but Hera spake, "Well do we know, son of Chronos, that thy might is beyond all bounds; nevertheless we pity the Greeks, lest they fill up the measure of their fate and die."

Then Zeus spake again, "To-morrow, Queen Hera, shalt thou see worse things than these; for great Hector will not cease from his slaying till the son of Peleus be roused by his ships, in the day when they shall fight about the dead Patroclus in the dark press of men."

And now the sun sank into the sea; wroth were the Trojans that the light should go, but to the Greeks welcome, much prayed for, came the night.

Then Hector called the men of Troy to an assembly. In his hand he held a spear eleven cubits long, with flaming point of bronze, and circled with gold; on it he leant and spake : —

"Give ear, ye Trojans, Dardans, and allies! I thought this day to destroy the hosts of the

Greeks and their ships, and so to return to Troy; but night hath hindered me. Let us yield to night, and take our meal. Unharness your horses and feed them. Fetch also from the city kine, and sheep, and wine, and bread, and store of fuel also, that we may burn many fires, lest, haply, the Greeks escape across the sea in the night. Not in peace shall they embark, but each shall carry away a wound to nurse at home that others may not seek to trouble the men of Troy with war. Also let the heralds make proclamation in the city, that the lads and the old men should guard the wall, and that every woman should light a great fire in her house, and that all should keep watch, lest an ambush should enter the city while the people are away. So much to-day; but to-morrow I will speak other words to you. In the morning will we arm ourselves, and wake the war beside the ships. Then shall I know whether Diomed will drive me from the wall, or I slay him with the spear. Would that I were immortal and held in honour as are the gods, as surely as to-morrow will bring ruin on the Greeks."

So Hector spake, and all the Trojans shouted their assent. They loosed their horses, and fetched provender from the city, and gathered store of fuel. All night long they sat high in hope; and as on some windless night the stars shine bright about the moon, and all the crags and dells are shown, and the tops of the hills also, and the depths of the sky are open, and all the stars appear, and the shepherd's heart is glad; so many showed the Trojan fires between the stream of Xanthus and the ships. A thousand fires were burning, and fifty sat in the glare of each; and the horses stood beside the chariots champing barley and spelt, and waited for the morn.

# CHAPTER XI.

## THE EMBASSY TO ACHILLES.

WHILE the Trojans watched with good hope, the Greeks were possessed with fear. And King Agamemnon was troubled beyond all others. He bade the heralds call every man to the assembly, bidding them severally without making proclamation. Gloomily they sat, and when the King rose up to speak, his tears dropped down, as the waters drop down a steep cliff-side from some spring which the sunshine toucheth not. Thus he spake: "O friends, lords and leaders of the Greeks, verily Zeus dealeth ill with me. Once he promised that I should take the city of Troy and so return home; but now he hath deceived me, bidding me go back dishonoured, having lost much people. Thus indeed do I now read his decree. Wherefore let us flee with our ships to the land of our fathers, for Troy we may not take."

Long time the chiefs kept silence, for they were out of heart; but at the last rose Diomed, and spake: "Be not wroth, O King, if I contend with this thy madness. Thou hast called me laggard and coward; whether I be so indeed the Greeks know well, both young and old. But to thee Zeus hath given lordship and the power of the sceptre above thy fellows; but courage he hath not given, and courage is best of all. Now if thine heart be bent upon return, go thou; the way is nigh, and thy ships are by the sea; but all the other Greeks will abide till they have taken Troy. Yea, and if these also will go, then we two, I and Sthenelus, will abide and fight till we make an end of the city, for it was the gods that sent us hither."

Then Nestor spake: "Thou art brave in war, son of Tydeus, and excellent in council above thy fellows. In what thou hast said none will gainsay thee. But now let us take our meal; and let sentinels watch along the trench. And do thou, son of Atreus, make a feast for thy chiefs, as is meet. And him who counsels thee most wisely thou must follow. Sorely do we need wise counsel, seeing that the enemy have so many fires near our ships. Verily this night will save our army or destroy."

So King Agamemnon called the chiefs to a feast; and when the feast was ended Nestor rose up and spake: " Zeus hath made thee King over many nations, that thou mayest deal wisely with them. Therefore it is thy part to listen to the word of another when he shall speak that which is profitable. Evil was the day, O King, when thou didst send and take the damsel Briseïs from the tent of Achilles. The chiefs of the Greeks consented not to thy deed. And I would fain have persuaded thee to forbear, but thou wouldst not hearken, but didst listen to the counsel of pride, working shame to the bravest of the people, and taking from him the reward of his labours. Let us therefore take thought how we may best appease him with noble gifts and pleasant words."

Then said King Agamemnon: " These are true words that thou hast spoken, old man. Truly I did as a fool that day, and I deny it not. For he that is loved of Zeus is of more worth than whole armies of men; and verily Zeus loveth this man, seeing that he putteth the Greeks to flight that he may do him honour. But even as I wronged him in my folly, so will I make amends, and give a recompense beyond all telling. And now I will declare before you all the gifts that I will give: seven tripods that the fire hath never touched, and ten talents of gold, and twenty shining caldrons, and twelve stout horses, that have won prizes in the race by fleetness of foot. No beggar were he, nor without store of precious gold, who should hold all that my horses have won for me. And seven women will I give him, skilled in excellent handiwork, daughters of Lesbos, fairer than all women else, whom I chose for my portion of the spoil in the day when he took Lesbos by the might of his arm. These will I give him, and with them the damsel Briseïs, even as I took her from him. And if the gods shall grant us to destroy the great city of Priam, then let him come when we divide the spoil, and choose for himself twenty women of Troy, the fairest there be after Argive Helen. And if he come again to the land of Greece, then shall he be my son, and I will honour him even as I honour Orestes. Three daughters have I in my palace at home, Chrysothemis, and Lao-dicé, and Iphianassa. Let him choose which of them he will, and take her, unbought by wooer's gift, to the hall of Peleus. Yea, and I will give with her a great dower also, such as man never yet gave to his daughter. Seven fair cities will I give him, with pasture-lands and vineyards, wherein dwell men that have many flocks and herds, who will honour him with gifts even as men honour a god, and will fulfil his commands. All this will I give him, if so be that he will cease from his anger. Let him yield; for only Death of all things that are yieldeth not, wherefore Death is abhorred of all men."

To him Nestor made answer: "No man may lightly esteem the gifts that thou givest to great Achilles. Come, therefore, let us choose men that they may go with all speed to his tent. Let Phœnix, who is beloved of Zeus, lead the way; and let Ajax the Greater and Ulysses go with him, and two heralds also.

And now let men bring water for our hands, and let all keep silence while we pray to Zeus, that he may have mercy upon us."

Then the heralds poured water on their hands, and filled the bowls full with wine. And, when they had made libation to the gods, they drank, and so came forth from the tent of the King. And Nestor charged them all, but chiefly Ulysses, of what they should say, and how they might best persuade the son of Peleus.

So they went by the shore of the sea; and, as they went, they made instant prayer to the god that shakes the earth that they might turn the heart of Achilles. And when they came to the ships of the Myrmidons, they found the King taking his pleasure with a harp, fairly wrought, with a crossbar of silver upon it, that he had taken from the spoil of Thebé-under-Placus, that was the city of King Eëtion. There he sat, delighting his soul with music, and sang the deeds of heroes of old time. And Patroclus sat over against him in silence, waiting till he should cease from his singing. Then the two chiefs came forward, Ulysses

THE EMBASSY TO ACHILLES.

leading the way, and stood before the face of Achilles; and Achilles leapt up in much amaze, holding the harp in his hand. And Patroclus rose also from his seat when he saw the twain. Then said Achilles, fleet of foot, " Welcome ye are, and right dear to me, for all my anger."

So spake Achilles, and led them forward; and he bade them sit on seats that were covered with coverlets of purple. Then said he to Patroclus, " Bring forth the biggest bowl, and mingle drinks of the strongest, for each man a cup, for I have not dearer friends than these that are come beneath my roof this day."

And Patroclus hearkened to his words. And afterwards he set before the heat of the fire a mighty fleshing-block; and he laid upon it the back of a sheep and of a fatted goat, and a hog's chine also rich with fat. And Automedon, that was charioteer to Achilles, held the flesh, and Achilles carved it. Well did he carve it, and spitted it upon spits, and Patroclus made the fire burn high. And when the flames had died away, he smoothed down the embers, and laid the spits with the flesh upon the spit-racks above them, sprinkling them first with salt. And when the flesh was broiled, he portioned it forth upon platters; and afterwards took bread, and set it upon the table in baskets. Then Achilles sat himself down over against Ulysses by the other wall of the tent. And Patroclus did sacrifice to the gods at his bidding, casting the first-fruits into the fire. After this the chiefs stretched forth their hands to the meat that lay ready before them. And when they had done with the desire for food and drink, Ajax nodded to Phœnix that he should speak; but Ulysses perceived it, and was beforehand with him, and filled a cup with wine, and pledged Achilles, and spake: " Hail, Achilles! No lack have we had of feasting before in the tent of King Agamemnon and now in thine; but it is not of feasting that we think this day; for we behold a sore destruction close at hand, and are afraid. Verily, we are in doubt whether or no we may save our ships, unless thou wilt gird on thy might again. For indeed this day the men of Troy and their allies came near to the ships to burn them with fire.

And Zeus shows them favourable signs, even lightning on the right hand. As for Hector, he rages furiously, trusting in Zeus, and cares not aught for god or man. Verily, even now is he praying that the morning may appear; for he vows that he will cut off their ensigns from our ships, — yea, and burn the ships with fire, and make havoc of the Greeks while they are dazed with the smoke of the burning. Sorely do I fear in my heart lest the god fulfil his threats, and doom us to perish here in Troy, far from the plains of Argos. Up, therefore, if thou art minded even now to save the Greeks! Delay not, lest thou repent hereafter, for there is no remedy for that which is done. Did not the old man Peleus, thy father, in the day when he sent thee from Phthia to King Agamemnon, give thee this commandment, saying: 'My son, Athené and Hera will give thee strength, if it be their will; but do thou restrain thy pride of heart, for gentleness is better than pride; and keep thee from strife, that the Greeks, both young and old, may honour thee the more'? So the old man gave thee commandment, but thou forgettest his words. Yet even now cease from thy anger. Verily, Agamemnon offereth thee worthy gifts, so that thou put away thy wrath — ten tripods that have not felt the fire, and ten talents of gold, and twenty shining caldrons, and twelve stout horses that have won much wealth for Agamemnon by fleetness of foot, and seven women, daughters of Lesbos, skilful in handiwork, and fairer than all their kind; and Briseïs herself he will restore to thee, even as he took her from thee. All these things will he give; and if we take the great city of Priam, twenty daughters of Troy, fairest of women, after Argive Helen. And when we shall go back to Greece, thou shalt have his daughter to wife, her whom thou shalt choose, and pay no gifts of wooing for her, but rather have such dowry as never king gave with his daughter before: seven cities shalt thou have, lying all of them near to the sea, a land of vineyards, and cornfields, whose folk shall pay thee tribute and honour. But if thou yet hate from thy heart Agamemnon and his gifts, then I pray thee have pity upon the Greeks, who will honour thee even as men honour a god. Hector, too, thou mayest slay, for he will come near thee in his madness, for he deems that there is not a man of all the Greeks that can stand against him."

To him Achilles, fleet of foot, made answer: "Son of Laertes, plain shall be my speech, setting forth my thought and the steadfast purpose of my heart; for I would not have you sit before me, seeking to coax me, one man this way and another another. As for the man that hideth one thing in his heart, and speaketh another with his lips, I hate him as I hate the gates of death. Tell me, why should a man do battle without ceasing with the foe? Surely it is a thankless work, for he that abideth at home hath equal share with him that ceaseth not from battle, and the coward hath like honour with the brave, and death cometh with equal foot to him that toileth not and to him that ceaseth not from toil. No profit have I had for all the tribulation that I have endured, ever staking my life in the battle. For even as a bird carrieth morsels to her unfledged brood, but herself fareth ill, so passed I many sleepless nights, and fought for many toilsome days. Twelve cities laid I waste, sailing thereto on ships, and eleven whereunto I journeyed by land, all in this fair land of Troy; and out of all I took many and fair possessions. And these I carried to King Agamemnon; and he, ever abiding at the ships, portioned out a few to others, but kept the most himself. And what he gave to the other princes or the host he left to them; but from me, only from me among all the Greeks, he took away the gift that he had given. Yea, he took from me the lady whom I loved. He took her; let him keep her, if he will. Why must the Greeks make war against the sons of Troy? Why did the sons of Atreus gather this host together, and lead them to this land? Was it not for fair-haired Helen's sake? Tell me, then, do the sons of Atreus alone of all men love their wives? Nay, but whosoever is good and sound of heart loveth his wife and cherisheth her, even as I loved mine, though I won her by my spear. He took her from me, and deceived me; let him not make trial of me again, for I know him well, and he shall not prevail with me. Let him take counsel now with thee, Ulysses, and with the other princes of the host, how he may keep from the ships the devouring fire. Many things hath he done without my help, building a wall and digging a ditch about it, both wide and deep, and setting stakes in the ditch; yet for all this can he not keep Hector from the ships. And yet, when I fought in the host of the Greeks, this Hector dared not set his army in array far from the walls, but scarce came to the Scæan gates and the fig tree. Once did he await me there to do battle, man against man, and scarce escaped my spear. But now, seeing that I have no mind to fight with him, I will do sacrifice to-morrow to Zeus and all the gods, and I will store my ships and launch them on the sea. Yea, to-morrow, right early in the morning, thou shalt see them, if thou wilt, sailing along the Hellespont, and my men toiling eagerly at the oar; and if the god that shaketh the earth grants me a fair journey, on the third morning shall I come to the fair land of Phthia. There is all the wealth that I left behind me when I came to Troy; and hence I shall carry with me yet more of gold and

bronze and iron, and fair women slaves, my
portion of the spoil.  My portion they are, but
my choicest gift King Agamemnon has taken
from me; he took it, having given it himself.
Never will I take counsel with him again, nor
bear him company in battle; once hath he
deceived me; let this suffice.  He shall not
beguile me again with lying speech.  And as
for his gifts, I scorn them; though he give me
tenfold, yea, twentyfold, all that he now hath
promised, though it be as the wealth of Thebes
that is in the land of Egypt, and than Thebes,
I ween, there is no wealthier city.  A hundred
gates it hath, and from each gate two hundred
warriors issue forth with horses and chariots.
Yea, verily, though he give me gifts as the
sand of the sea for multitude, he shall not persuade me, till he shall have endured like bitter-
ness of soul with mine.  And his daughter I
will not wed — no, not though she be as fair as
goiden Aphrodité, and match Athené of the
flashing eyes in skill of handiwork.  Let him
choose him, forsooth, from among the Greeks
some kinglier son-in-law than I, and for me, if
the gods bring me safe to my home, Peleus

shall choose a wife. Many maidens, daughters of princes, are there in Hellas and in Phthia. Of these I will wed whomsoever I will. Often, indeed, in time past was I moved to take for me a wife, to be my helpmeet, that I might have joy with her of the possessions of Peleus, my father. For all the wealth that was stored in the city of Troy, in the days of peace, before the Greeks came thither, and all the treasure that is laid up in the temple of Apollo the Archer that is in the city of Delphi — all this I count as nothing in comparison of life. For a man may take cattle and sheep for spoil, and he may buy tripods and horses; but the life of a man, when it hath once passed from out his lips, he may not win back by spoiling or by buying. And to me my mother, even Thetis, the goddess of the silver foot, hath unfolded my doom. A double doom it is. If I abide in this land and fight against the city of Troy, then shall I return no more to my native country, but my name shall live forever; but if I go back to my home, then my fame shall be taken from me, but I shall live long and see not the grave. Therefore I go, and verily I counsel you all to go, for Troy ye never shall take as ye desire, seeing that Zeus, who seeth all things before, holdeth over it his hand, and her sons are a valiant folk. And now go your way; carry back this answer to the princes of the Greeks: 'Devise ye in your hearts some better counsel whereby ye may keep the men of Troy from your ships; for this counsel availeth naught, so fierce is my anger.' But let the old man Phœnix abide with me in my tent to-night, that he may sail in my ship on the morrow. Verily he shall sail, if he will; but I will not take him by force."

Thus spake Achilles. And the chiefs sat still and held their peace, marvelling at his speech, so vehement was he in his denying. But at the last the old man Phœnix made answer. With many tears he spake, for he was sore afraid lest the ships of the Greeks should perish: " If indeed thou art minded to depart, and carest not to save the ships from devouring fire, how can I endure to be left alone of thee? For the old man Peleus made me thy teacher, both of words and of deeds, in the day when he sent thee forth from the land of Phthia to King Agamemnon, a stripling without knowledge of war or of counsel. Therefore I will not leave thee, no, not if the gods would take from me my years, and make me young as I was when I left the land of Hellas. Hellas I left because I had angered the old man, my father, and he cursed me, calling instantly on the Furies that never son of mine should sit upon his knees. Thus he prayed, and the gods hearkened to him, even Zeus that rules the dead and awful Persephoné. Then was I minded to slay him with the sword; but some god kept me back, putting it in my heart that I should be called the murderer of my father throughout the land of Hellas. But I was purposed not to abide in his dwelling any more. Then came comrades and kinsmen with many prayers, and would have kept me. Nine days they slew fat sheep and oxen, and broiled the swine's flesh in the fire, and wine they drank without stint from the old man's jars. Nine nights they slept about me, keeping watch by turn, and the fires burned continually, one in the cloister of the court, and one in the porch before the chamber doors. But when the tenth night came, and darkness was over all, I brake the chamber doors for all their cunning fastening, and, coming forth, leapt over the courtyard fence, and neither watchman nor handmaid marked me. Far over the land of Hellas I fled, and came to Phthia, to King Peleus. And Peleus received me with a kindly heart, and cherished me as a father cherisheth his son, even the heir of his possessions. Yea, and he made me rich, and gave me people to be under me, and I ruled the Dolopes that dwelt in the uttermost border of Phthia. And thee, Achilles, did I rear to the stature that thou hast. With no man but me wouldst thou go unto the feast, or take thy meat in the hall; but I set thee upon my knees, and cut the sa-voury morsel for thee from the dish, and put the wine-cup to thy lips. Many a tunic hast thou stained for me, sputtering forth the wine upon it. Much have I suffered, and much toiled for thee; for child of mine own I had not, and thou wast to me as a son, Achilles, to cherish me in my need. And now, I pray thee, rule thy anger, for it becometh thee not to keep a ruthless heart. Even the gods are turned from their purpose, and they are more honourable and mightier than thou. Yea, men turn them with incense and drink-offering, and burnt-offering and prayer, if so be that one has transgressed against them. Moreover, Prayers are the daughters of Zeus; halt are they, and wrinkled, and with eyes that look askance, and they follow ever in the steps of Sin. Strong is Sin, and fleet of foot, and far outrunneth them all, and goeth before over all the earth, working harm to men ; nevertheless, Prayers follow behind to heal the harm. And whosoever shall reverence these daughters of Zeus when they come near unto him, him they bless, and accept his petitions ; but when one denieth them and refuseth them in the hardness of his heart, then they depart and make supplication to Zeus that he may perish. Take heed, therefore, Achilles, that thou pay to the daughters of Zeus such reverence as becometh a righteous man. If, indeed, King Agamemnon offered thee not gifts in the present, and promised thee more hereafter, I would not bid thee cease from thy anger, no, not to save the Greeks in their distress.   But now he gives thee much and promises thee more, and hath sent his ambassadors, the men that are the noblest of the host, and withal dearest to thee.   Refuse not, therefore, their words.   For the heroes also in former days when fierce anger came upon them could be turned with gifts and persuaded by prayers. Listen, now, to this tale that I will tell.   The Curetes in old time fought against the fair city of Calydon, and the Ætolians defended it, and there was war between them.   For Artemis had brought a plague upon them, being wroth because King Œneus offered her not the firstfruits.   The other gods had sacrifice, but to the daughter of Zeus he made no offering, whether he forgot the matter or heeded her not.   And the Queen of Arrows was very wroth, and sent a great wild boar with long white tusks into the land, that laid waste gardens and orchards.   But Meleager, son of Œneus, slew the beast, having first gathered many hunters and dogs, for only of many could he be slain, so mighty was he, and so many did he bring to the funeral fires.   And when he was slain much trouble arose about his head and shaggy hide, for the Curetes and Ætolians contended together who should have them. Now, so long as Meleager fought in the host of the Ætolians, so long it fared ill with the Curetes, till they dared not to come without the walls of their city, for all that they were many in number. But after a while he went no more with the host of the Ætolians to battle, but tarried at home with his wedded wife, Cleopatra, daughter of Marpessa and of Idas, that was the strongest of mortal men. Strongest he was, and dared to stand face to face with his bow against the archer Apollo. For Idas had carried away Marpessa from the halls of her father, and when Apollo would have taken her from him, he stood against him; so the two fought together; but Zeus commanded that the damsel should choose between them. So she chose the hero rather than the god, for, she said, ' He will be faithful to me.' And now Meleager tarried at home, being wroth with his mother, Althæa; and the cause of his anger was this: He was minded to give the spoils of the wild boar to the fair huntress, Atalanta, that came from the land of Arcadia ; and when the brethren of his mother would have taken them from her, he slew them. Then his mother, being grieved for her brethren, knelt on her knees upon the ground, and beat it with her hands and wept, praying instantly to Pluto and Persephoné, that they should bring her son to death. And the Fury that walketh in darkness and hath no pity upon men, heard her from the pit. And now there was the din of foemen about the gates; and the elders of the Ætolians besought him, sending the priests of the gods, the holiest that there were, to come forth and defend them, and promised him a goodly gift. For they bade him choose for himself from the plain of Ætolia, even where it was richest, a fair domain, of ploughland half and of vineyard half. Then the old man Œneus besought him, standing on the threshold of his chamber and shaking the doors. Also his sisters and his mother besought him, but he refused the more vehemently. And his comrades came that were nearest and dearest of all men to him, but they prevailed not with him. But at the last, when the enemy were now battering the door of his chamber, and were climbing on the towers, and burning the fair city with fire, then the fair Cleopatra arose and besought him with many tears that he would save the people; for she told him all the woes that come upon them whose city is taken by their enemies, how that the warriors are slain, and the streets wasted with fire, and the children and women led into captivity. Then was his spirit stirred within him, and he rose from his place, and put his shining arms upon him, and saved the Ætolians from destruction. He saved them; but the gifts, many and fair, which they had promised, they gave him not. But let not thy thoughts, my son, be as the thoughts of Meleager. It would be an ill task for thee to save the ships when they are already burning. Come, therefore, for the gifts which the King will give thee; come, and the Greeks will honour thee as men honour a god. But this honour wilt thou miss if thou receive not the gifts, yea, though thou save us from the men of Troy."

To him Achilles, fleet of foot, made answer: " Phœnix, my father, such honour as this I need not; already have I honour enough by the giving of Zeus. And this also I say to thee. Trouble me no more with thy tears and thy lamenting while thou seekest to serve King Agamemnon. Favour him not, lest thou be hated of me, who love thee now. Rather shouldst thou vex the man who vexeth me. Come, therefore, and take the half of my kingdom. Let these take my message to the King, but abide thou here with me; and when the day shall come we will take counsel together whether we will tarry here or depart."

Then Achilles nodded to Patroclus, that he should spread a couch for the old man Phœnix, that so the other twain might depart without delay. Then said Ajax, the son of Telamon: "Let us depart, Ulysses. I trow that we shall accomplish naught this day. Let us, therefore, take back the tidings, evil though they be, to them that wait for us. As for Achilles, he hath wrought his soul to fury, and he seeketh not of the love of his comrades, or of the honour wherewith they honoured him above all others in the host. And yet a man will take fit recompense at the hand of him who hath slain his brother or his son. He taketh it, and his anger is appeased — and the shedder of blood abides in peace in his own land. But thou keepest thy anger forever, and all for a damsel's sake. Look! we offer thee seven damsels, very fair to see, and many gifts besides. Think thee, and have also some thought for thy guest, for we are under thy roof, and would fain be thy friends, dearer to thee than all besides."

Then said Achilles: "Thy speech seemeth to please me well, great son of Telamon. Nevertheless, my heart swells with wrath, when I remember how the son of Atreus shamed me before all the people, as though I was some stranger nothing worth. But go and take my message. I will not arise to the battle till Hector shall come as he slays the Greeks even to the tents of the Myrmidons, and shall encircle their ships with fire. But when he shall come to my tent and to my ships, then I ween shall he be stayed, for all that he is eager for battle."

Then Ajax and Ulysses departed, and told the message of Achilles to King Agamemnon.

# CHAPTER XII.

### THE ADVENTURE OF ULYSSES AND DIOMED.

THE other chiefs of the Greeks slept that night; but King Agamemnon slept not; sore troubled was he in heart. For when he looked towards Troy, and saw the many fires, and heard the sound of flute and pipe and the murmur of men, he was astonished; and when he looked towards the ships he groaned, and tare his hair, thinking what evil might come to the people. Then it seemed good to him to seek counsel from Nestor, if haply they two might devise some useful device. So he arose, and drew his coat about his breast, and bound the sandals on his feet, and wrapped a tawny lion's hide about him, and took a spear in his hand.

To Menelaüs also came no sleep that night. So he arose, and wrapped a leopard's skin about him, and put on his head a cap of bronze, and took a spear in his hand, and went to seek his brother.

He found him arming by his ship, and said: "Why armest thou? Wilt thou send some one to spy out the doings of the Trojans? I fear me much that no man will undertake the task to go alone, for it is a daring deed."

To him replied King Agamemnon: "We have need of good counsel, my brother, that we may save the people. Truly the mind of Zeus is changed; for never hath a man wrought such destruction in one day as did Hector on the Greeks, and yet he is not the son either of goddess or of god. But now run thou to Ajax and Idomeneus, and call them to the council, and I will go to Nestor."

So the chiefs were gathered to the council. First of all they went to the company of them that watched the camp. These they found not sleeping but awake, like to dogs that hear the sound of some wild beast in the wood, so did the watch look towards the plain, thinking to hear the sound of the feet of the Trojans.

Gladly did old Nestor see them, and spake,

saying, "Such be your watch, my children, lest we become a prey to our enemies."

Then he hasted to cross the trench, and with him went the other princes. In an open space they sat down that was clear of dead, even where Hector had turned back from slaying the Greeks.

And Nestor rose and said: "Is there now a man who will go among the sons of Troy, and see what they are minded to do? Great honour will he win, and gifts withal."

Then Diomed said, "I am ready to go, but I would fain have some one with me. To have a companion gives comfort and courage, and, indeed, two wits are better than one to take counsel and to foresee."

And many were willing to go with Diomed. Ajax the Greater and Ajax the Less, and Meriones, and Thrasymedes, old Nestor's son (and no one, indeed, wished it more than he), and Menelaüs and Ulysses.

But Agamemnon said, "Choose the best man, O Diomed, and regard not the birth or rank of any." This he said, fearing for his brother Menelaüs.

And Diomed answered: " Nay, but if I may choose, whom should I choose rather than the wise Ulysses?  Brave is he, and prudent, and Athené loves him well."

But Ulysses said: " Praise me not overmuch, nor blame me.  Only let us go, for the night is far spent."

So these two armed themselves.  Diomed took a two-edged sword and a shield, and a helmet without a crest, and Ulysses a bow and a quiver and a sword, and a helmet of hide with the white teeth of a wild boar about it. Then both prayed to Athené that she would help them, and after that .they went through the darkness like to two lions, trampling over dead bodies and arms and blood.

But Hector, meanwhile, was thinking on the same things, for he called the chiefs to a council and said: " Who now will go and spy among the Greeks, and see what they purpose to do on the morrow, and whether they are keeping watch through the night.  A goodly reward shall he have, even a chariot and horses, the best that there are in the camp of the Greeks."

K

Then stood up a certain Dolon, the son of the herald Eumedes. Ill-favoured was he, but a swift runner, the only son of his father, but he had five sisters. He said: —

"I will go, Hector; but come, lift up thy sceptre, and swear to me that thou wilt give me the chariot and the horses of Achilles."

So Hector sware to him, but it was an idle oath. And Dolon took his bow, and a helmet of grisly wolf-skin, and a sharp spear, and went his way in haste. But Ulysses saw him, and said: —

"Here cometh a man, Diomed, but whether he be a spy or a spoiler of the dead I know not. Let him pass by a space that we may take him. If he outrun us, press him with thy spear towards the ships; only let him not turn back to the city."

So they lay down among the dead, a little out of the way, and Dolon passed by them unknowing; but when he had gone a little space they ran upon him. For a while he stood hearkening to their steps, for he thought that Hector had sent comrades to call him back. But when they were a spear's throw from him, or less, he knew them for foes and fled. And just as two dogs follow a fawn or a hare, so they two ran, pursuing Dolon. And when he had well-nigh reached the trench, for they kept him that he should not turn back to the city, Diomed rushed forward and cried: —

"Stay, or I will slay thee with my spear."

And he threw the spear, and smote not the man indeed, for that he wished not, but made it pass over his shoulder, so that it stood in the ground before him. Then Dolon stood trembling and pale, and with teeth chattering with fear. And the two heroes, breathing hard, came up and laid hands on him. And he said, weeping: —

" Hold me to ransom; much gold and bronze and iron will my father give, if he hear that I am a prisoner at the ships."

Then said the wise Ulysses: " Be of good cheer, and think not of death. But tell us truly, why wast thou coming hither through the darkness? To spoil the dead, or, at Hector's bidding, to spy out our affairs at the ships, or on some errand of thine own? "

And Dolon answered, " Hector persuaded

me, promising to give me the horses and chariot of Achilles, and he bade me go and spy out what ye purposed to do on the morrow, and whether ye were keeping watch in the night."

And Ulysses smiled and said: "Surely it was a great reward that thy soul desired. The horses of Achilles are grievous for any man to drive, save for him that is born of a goddess. But tell me, where is Hector, and where are the watches of the sons of Troy?"

Then Dolon answered: "Hector holds council with the chiefs by the tomb of Ilus. But as for the army, there are no watches set, save only where be the Trojans themselves. But as for the allies, they sleep secure, and trust to the Trojans to watch for them, seeing that they have not wives or children near."

Then Ulysses asked, "Do they sleep, then, among the Trojans, or apart?"

"Next to the sea," said Dolon, "are the men of Caria and Pæonia, and close to these the men of Lycia and Mysia and Phrygia. But if ye wish to enter the camp, lo! apart from all are some newcomers, Thracians, with Rhesus,

DIOMED AND ULYSSES RETURNING WITH THE SPOILS OF RHESUS.

their King. Never have I seen horses so fair and tall as his. Whiter are they than snow, and swifter than the winds. But do ye now send me to the ships, or, if ye will, bind me and leave me here."

But Diomed said: "Think not to escape, Dolon, though thy news is good; for then wouldst thou come again to spy out our camp or to fight. But if I slay thee, thou wilt trouble the Greeks no more."

So he slew him, and took from him his arms, hanging them on a tamarisk tree, and made a mark with reeds and tamarisk boughs, that they might know the place as they came back. So they went on across the plain and came to where the men of Thrace lay sleeping, and by each man were his arms in fair array, and his horses; but in the midst lay King Rhesus, with his horses tethered to the chariot-rail. Then Diomed began to slay. As a lion rushes on a flock, so rushed he on the men of Thrace. Twelve he slew, and as he slew them Ulysses dragged them out of the way, that there might be a clear road for the horses, lest they should start back, fearing the dead bodies, for they were not used to war. And the thirteenth was King Rhesus himself, who panted in his sleep, for an evil dream was on him. And meanwhile Ulysses drove the horses out of the encampment, smiting them with his bow, for he had not thought to take the whip out of the chariot. Then he whistled, making a sign to Diomed that he should come, for Diomed lingered, doubting whether he might not slay yet more. But Athené whispered in his ear : —

" Think of thy return, lest haply some god rouse the Trojans against thee."

And, indeed, Apollo was even then rousing them. For Hippocoön, cousin to King Rhesus, awoke, and seeing the place of the horses empty and his comrades slain, groaned aloud, and called to the King, and the Trojans were roused, and flocked together with tumult and shouting. But Diomed and Ulysses meanwhile had mounted the horses, and were riding to the ships. Glad were their comrades to see them safe returned, and praised them much for all that they had done.

# CHAPTER XIII.

## THE VALIANT DEEDS OF AGAMEMNON.

WHEN the next day dawned, King Agamemnon called the Greeks to battle. And first he donned his arms; about his breast he put the corselet which Cinyras of Cyprus gave him; twelve bands it had of dark iron, and twelve of gold, and of tin twenty, and on either side three dragons upright, stretching up to the neck, with many colours, as the rainbow which Zeus setteth in the clouds to be a sign to men. From his shoulder he hung his flashing sword with bosses of gold and silver scabbard; and on his arm he put his shield, ankle-long, with a Gorgon head, dreadful to look upon, in the midst, and Fear and Flight on either side. Rimmed with silver was the shield, and wrought upon the rims in iron a dragon with three heads growing from a single neck. Last he took two spears, one in either hand; and Athené and Hera thundered as he went to do him honour.

On the other side Hector set in order the men of Troy. As a baleful star now shineth from the clouds, and now is hidden, so Hector now shone among the foremost ranks, and now ordered the rearward.

Then the men of Troy and the Greeks leapt upon each other. As reapers reap in a rich man's field, making the barley and the wheat fall in long swathes, so did the Trojans and the Greeks slay one another. So long as the day was waxing the battle was equal, and the people fell alike on either side; but at noon, at the hour when he that cutteth wood among the hills groweth weary of his work and craveth for food, then the Greeks with a great onset brake the Trojan line, and Agamemnon leapt first into the breach. First he slew two men in one chariot, Bienor and his charioteer; and next to these two sons of Priam, Isus and Antiphus. These two Achilles had taken aforetime as they fed their flocks on the slopes of Ida, and had let them go for a ransom. Now Agamemnon came upon them, and he knew them, having seen them before at the ships. One he smote upon the breast with his spear, the other on his ear with his sword. Even as a lion comes upon the young of a doe, and crusheth them in his teeth, and the mother cannot help them, though she be near, but flieth trembling through the wood, so did these two perish, and none of the Trojans dared to help them, but rather fled themselves.

Next to these Agamemnon found the sons of Antimachus. These two he took alive in their chariot, for they had dropped the reins, and stood helpless before him, crying out that he should spare them, and take ransom, for that Antimachus their father had much gold and bronze and iron in his house, and would gladly buy them back alive. Now Antimachus had taken a bribe from Prince Paris, and had given counsel to the Trojans that they should not give back the fair Helen. So when King Agamemnon heard them, he said: "Nay, but if ye be sons of Antimachus, who counselled the men of Troy that they should slay Menelaüs when he came an ambassador to their city, ye shall die for your father's sin." So he slew them both, and, leaving them, still rushed on, driving back the Trojans, even to the walls of their city, and the Greeks came after him, and footman slew footman, and horseman, horseman. As a fire falleth on a wood, and sweepeth it away, so Agamemnon fell upon the men of Troy, and swept them before him. Past the Tomb of Ilus, and past the wild fig tree in the plain, they fled, and the King followed hard upon them, shouting aloud. But when they came to the Scæan gate they turned and stood, and the battle was renewed.

Then spake Zeus to Iris, saying: " Get thee away, swift Iris, and bear this word to Hector. So long as he shall see King Agamemnon laying waste the ranks of men, so long let him hold back from the battle. But when the King shall be wounded with spear or arrow, and shall leap from his chariot, then let him advance, and I will give him strength to slay till he shall come to the ships, and the sun shall set."

So he came, and told these words to Hector.

And when Hector heard them, he leapt from his chariot, and went up and down the ranks of Troy, strengthening them for the fight. And the two hosts stood, and faced each other.

Then did King Agamemnon slay the two sons of Antenor. First he slew Iphidamas, who had been reared in his grandsire's halls, the father of fair Theano, Antenor's wife. There he had married a wife, giving for her many gifts; a hundred oxen he paid in hand, and a thousand sheep and goats he promised; but little joy he had, for while yet a bridegroom he came to fight for Troy, and now the King slew him. First Agamemnon threw his spear, but missed his cast; then Antenor's son smote the King upon the girdle, beneath the corselet, leaning his weight upon the blow; but he pierced not the girdle, for the spear point came full upon the silver, and turned aside as it had been lead. Then the King caught the spear, and wrenched it from his hand, and smote him a deadly blow upon the neck.

But Coön, Antenor's first-born son, was grieved for his brother, and standing sideways, so that the King saw him not, he stabbed him in the middle of the arm, beneath the elbow, and the spear pierced it through. The King started, yet ceased not from battle, but as Coön dragged his brother by the foot out of the press, calling upon the chiefs to help, then Agamemnon smote him with the spear, beneath the shield, and drove him to the ground, and after smote off his head with the sword. Thus did Agamemnon slay the two sons of Antenor.

For a while, while the wound was warm, the King fought as before; but when it grew cold and stiff, great pain came upon him, and he leapt into his chariot and bade the charioteer drive him to the ships, for that he could fight no more.

# CHAPTER XIV.

## THE WOUNDING OF THE CHIEFS.

WHEN Hector saw that Agamemnon had departed from the battle, he called aloud to the Trojans and the allies: "Come on, and play the man. The leader of the Greeks is gone; and Zeus giveth the honour unto me."

So he stirred the spirit within them. As a hunter setteth his dogs on a wild boar or a lion in the field, so did Hector set the men of Troy upon the Greeks, and he himself went among the foremost, and plunged into the battle as a storm cometh down upon the sea. Many valiant men did he slay, till Ulysses called to Diomed: "Son of Tydeus, have we forgotten our courage? Come hither, and stand by me; it were shame if Hector should take our ships."

Strong Diomed made answer, "I will, indeed, abide with thee; but it will fare ill with us if Zeus give the mastery to the men of Troy rather than to us."

So he spake, and slew a man, and Ulysses another; and afterwards they slew two apiece, making head against the men of Troy, and the Greeks, as they fled from Hector, gladly took breath and turned again.

Hector was quick to see what they did, and he came upon them with a cry, and the companies of Troy followed after him. But when Diomed saw him, he was afraid, and said to Ulysses, "See, mighty Hector cometh against us; let us be firm and stand against him."

And even as he spake he cast his spear, nor missed his aim. On the helmet he smote Hector; but the spear glanced from the bronze, nor wounded the flesh; for the helmet which Apollo had given him saved him. But he staggered under the blow, falling on his knee, and darkness came over his eyes. And when Diomed came after his spear, far through the foremost ranks, to where it had lighted on the ground, then Hector, breathing again, leapt upon his car, and drove into the midst of the host, avoiding death.

Then Diomed, as he rushed on, with his spear in his hand, cried aloud: "Dog, thou hast escaped from death once more; but mischief came near thee. Apollo hath saved thee, to whom doubtless thou prayest ere thou came into the press of war. But some time I will slay thee, if only some god will help."

And he turned to slay the men of Troy. But while he spoiled the son of Pæon, whom he had slain ere Hector came against him, Paris, who was in hiding behind the pillar on the Tomb of Ilus, drew his bow, and smote him with an arrow through the ankle of the right foot. Loud he boasted of his aim. "Only," he said, "I would that I had pierced thee in the loin; then hadst thou troubled the sons of Troy no more."

But Diomed answered: "Small good were thy bow to thee, cowardly archer, if thou shouldst dare to meet me face to face. And as for this graze on my foot, I care no more than if a woman or child had smitten me. Not such the wounds I deal; as for those that meet my spear in the battle, I think that they are dearer to the fowls of the air than to women in the chamber."

Then Ulysses stood before him, while he

drew the arrow out of his foot. Grievous was the smart of the wound, for all his brave words. Wherefore he leapt into his chariot, and bade drive in haste to the ships; and Ulysses stood alone, and none of the Greeks stood by him, for all were sore afraid. Then spake he to himself: —

"What shall I do? It were much evil to fly before these many foes, and yet worse evil were I to be caught and slain, for truly Zeus hath sent great fear upon the Greeks. But why talk I thus? 'Tis only the coward that draweth back from the war; the brave man standeth whether he smite or be smitten."

And as he spake, the Trojans came about him as men with dogs come about a wild boar who stands at bay, gnashing his white teeth. Fiercely Ulysses stood at bay, and slew five chiefs of fame. But one of them, Socus by name, before he fell, wounded him on the side, scraping the flesh from the ribs. High spurted the blood from the wound, and the Trojans shouted to see it. Then Ulysses cried aloud for help; three times he cried, and Mene-laüs heard him, and called to Ajax, saying: —

"O Ajax, I hear the voice of Ulysses; and he shouteth as if the men of Troy had compassed him about, and he was left alone. Come, therefore, let us help him, lest he come to harm, and the Greeks have a heavy loss!"

Thus he spake, and led the way, and Ajax followed him; and when they came to Ulysses, the Trojans had beset him, even as the jackals beset a long-horned hart among the hills, which a hunter hath wounded with an arrow from the bow. From the hunter he flieth, while the wound is warm, but when he groweth weak the jackals tear him. Then cometh a lion, and the jackals flee. So fled the Trojans when Ajax came and stood beside Ulysses. Then Menelaüs took Ulysses by the hand, and led him from out the throng.

Then Ajax leapt upon the Trojans and slew many, scouring the plain, and killing horse and man. But Hector knew not of it, for he fought upon the left of the battle by the banks of Scamander, where old Nestor and Idomeneus of Crete kept up the battle for the Greeks. Nor had these given way but that Paris, husband of Helen, stayed Machaon from the fight, wounding him on the right shoulder with a three-pointed arrow. Therefore spake Idomeneus to Nestor, "Quick, Nestor, mount thy chariot and take Machaon with thee, and drive quickly to the ships, for the life of a physician is as the lives of many men!"

So Nestor mounted on his chariot, and Machaon stood beside him. He touched the horses, and they flew right willingly to the ships.

Meanwhile Cebriones, Hector's charioteer, said to Hector: "We two fight with the Greeks upon the outskirts of the battle; but yonder Ajax confounds the men of Troy. Let us, therefore, turn the chariot thither, for there is the sorest need."

So he spake, and lashed the horses. And when they felt the whip, they bare the chariot swiftly on, over shields and bodies of men, and the axle beneath and the chariot sides were bespattered with blood. Up and down the ranks went Hector, but he avoided the mighty Ajax. But Zeus the Father sent fear upon Ajax, and he cast his seven-fold shield behind his shoulders, and turned his back, yet again and again he faced round upon the enemy. As when an ass turns into a field and eats the standing corn, and the children beat him with sticks, but their strength is feebleness, and the sticks are broken on his back, for he is slow to go, nor do they drive him out, though with much pains, till he has eaten his fill, thus did the men of Troy hang upon Ajax, and thrust at him with their lances. And now he would turn about and check them, and now he would draw back; but ever he kept them from the ships.

And when Eurypylus saw him thus beset he went and stood beside him, and smote a Trojan chief and slew him. But when he leapt upon the dead man and began to spoil him of his arms, then Paris drew his bow upon him, and pierced him with an arrow in the right thigh.

Then Eurypylus called aloud, " O friends, leaders of the Greeks, come, and keep the day of death from Ajax, for he is sore beset."

Then the Greeks stood close about him, and Ajax turned about and stood when he came to the ranks of his fellows.

Now Achilles was standing on the stern of his ship, looking at the war, and he saw Nestor carrying Machaon in his chariot to the ships. Then he called to Patroclus, and Patroclus, who was in the tent, came forth; but it was an evil hour for him. Then said Achilles : —

" Now will the Greeks soon come, methinks, praying for help, for their need is sore. But go and see who is this whom Nestor is taking to the ships. His shoulders are the shoulders of Machaon, but I saw not his face, so swift the horses passed me by."

Then Patroclus ran.

Meanwhile Nestor brought Machaon into his tent. There Hecamedé of the beautiful locks, whom the Greeks had given to Nestor from the spoils of Tenedos, mixed them a posset. First she placed a table, and set on it a charger of bronze, with a leek that giveth savour to drink, and yellow honey, and barley meal. After that she brought a bowl; four handles it had, pair and pair, and over each pair twin doves that seemed to peck. A man might scarce lift it from the table when it was full, but Nestor raised it easily. Into the bowl the dame poūred Pramnian wine, and shredded on it cheese of goat's milk, and scattered the barley meal. And when the mess was ready, she bade them drink. So they drank, and delighted their souls with talk. But Patroclus stood in the door. But when old Nestor saw him, he went and took him by the hand, and would have had him sit down. But Patroclus would not, saying: —

"Stay me not. I came but to see who is this that thou hast brought wounded from the battle. And now I see that it is Machaon. Therefore I will return; for thou knowest what manner of man is Achilles, that he is hasty and swift to blame."

Then said Nestor: "But what careth Achilles for the Greeks? or why doth he ask who are wounded? But, O Patroclus, dost thou mind the day when I and Ulysses came to the house of Peleus, and how that thy father Menætius was there, and how we feasted in the hall; and when the feast was finished told our errand, for we were gathering the heroes for the war against the sons of Troy? Right willing were ye two to come, and many counsels did the old men give you. Then to Achilles Peleus said that he should always be foremost in the host, but to thee thy father Menætius spake: 'Achilles is nobler born than thou, and stronger far; but thou art older. Do thou therefore counsel him well, when there is need.' But this thou forgettest, Patroclus. Hear, then, what I say. It may be that Achilles will not go forth to the battle. But let him send thee forth, and the Myrmidons with thee, and let him put his arms upon thee, so that the sons of Troy be affrighted, thinking that he is in the battle, and we shall have breathing space."

Then Patroclus turned to run to Achilles, but as he ran he met Eurypylus, who spake to him : —

"Small hope is there now for the Greeks, seeing that all their bravest chiefs lie wounded at the ships. But do thou help me, for thou knowest all the secrets of healing, seeing that the wise Cheiron himself taught thee."

Then Patroclus answered, "I am even now on my way to tell these things to Achilles, but thee I may not leave in thy trouble."

So he took him to his tent, and cut out the
arrow from his thigh, washing the wound with
water, and putting on it a bitter, healing root,
so that the pain was stayed and the blood
stanched.

## CHAPTER XV.

### THE BATTLE AT THE WALL.

Now by this time the Trojans were close upon the trench. But the horses stood on the brink, fearing to leap it, for it was broad and deep, and the Greeks had put great stakes therein. Thus said Polydamas:—

"Surely, Hector, this is madness that we strive to cross the trench in our chariots, for it is broad and deep, and there are great stakes therein. Look, too, at this: even if we should be able to cross it, how will the matter stand? If, indeed, it be the pleasure of Zeus that the Greeks should perish utterly — it will be well. But if they turn upon us and pursue us, driving us back from the ships, then shall we not be able to return. Wherefore let us leave our chariots here upon the brink, and go on foot against the wall."

So they went in five companies, of whom Hector led that which was bravest and largest,

and with him were Polydamas and Cebriones.
And the next Paris commanded. And of the
third Helenus and Deïphobus were leaders,
and with them was Asius, the son of Hyrtacus,
from Arisbé. And the fourth followed Æneas,
the valiant son of Anchises. But of the allies
Sarpedon was the leader, and with him were
Glaucus and Asteropæus. And in each company they joined shield to shield, and so went
against the Greeks. Nor was there one of
them but hearkened to the counsel of Polydamas when he bade them leave their chariots
by the trench, save Asius only. But Asius
drove his chariot right up to that gate which
was on the left hand in the wall. Now the
gates chanced to be open, for the warders had
opened them, if so any of the Greeks that fled
might save themselves within them. Now the
warders were two mighty heroes of the race of
the Lapithæ, Polypœtes and Leonteus; and
these, when they saw Asius and his company
coming, went without and stood in front of the
gates, just as two wild boars stand at bay
against a crowd of men and dogs. And all
the while they that stood on the wall threw

heavy stones which fell, thick as the snow-flakes fall in the winter, on the men of Troy, and loud rang the helmets and the shields. And many fell wounded to the death, nor could Asius, for all his fury, win his way into the walls. But where, at another of the gates, Hector led the way, there appeared a strange marvel in the skies, for an eagle was bearing in his claws a great snake, which it had taken as a prey. But the snake fought fiercely for its life, and writhed itself about, even till it bit the eagle on the breast. Whereupon the eagle dropped it into the midst of the host, and fled with a loud cry. Then Polydamas, the wise counsellor, came near to Hector and said: —

"Now it will be well that we should not follow these Greeks to their ships. For I take it that this marvel that we have seen is a sign to us. For as this eagle had caught in his claws a snake, but held it not, dropping it before it could bear it to her young, so shall it fare with us. For we shall drive the Greeks to their ships, yet shall not subdue them, but shall return in disorder by the way that we

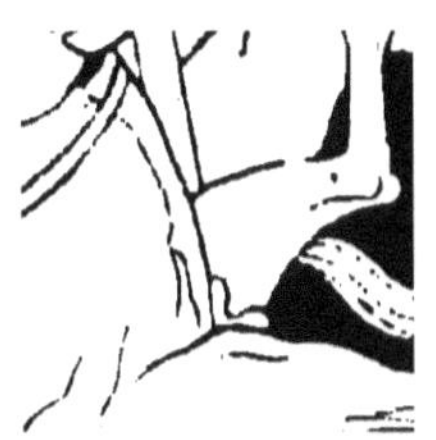

came, leaving full many of our comrades behind us."

But Hector frowned, and answered: " Nay, but this is ill counsel, Polydamas. For if thou sayest this from thy heart, surely the gods have changed thy wisdom into foolishness. Dost thou bid me forget the command of Zeus the Thunderer, and take heed to birds, how they fly? Little care I whether they go to the east or to the west, to the right or to the left. Surely there is but one sign for a brave man, that he be fighting for his fatherland. Wherefore take thou heed; for if thou holdest back from the war, or holdest back any other, lo! I will smite thee with my spear."

Then he sprang forward, and the men of Troy followed him with a shout. And Zeus sent down from Ida a great blast of wind which bore the dust of the plain straight to the ships, troubling the hearts of the Greeks. Then the Trojans sought to drag down the battlements from the wall, and to wrench up the posts which had been set to strengthen it. Nor did the Greeks give way, but they joined shield to shield, and fought for the wall. And foremost among them were Ajax the Greater and Ajax the Less. Just as the snow falls in mid-winter, when the winds are hushed, and the mountain-tops are covered, and the plains and the dwellings of men and the very shores of the sea, up to the waves' edge, so thickly fell the stones which the Greeks showered from the wall against the men of Troy, and which these again threw upon the Greeks. But still Hector and his men availed not to break through the gate. But at the last Zeus stirred up the heart of his own son, Sarpedon. Holding his shield before him he went, and he shook in either hand a spear. As goes a lion, when hunger presses him sore, against a stall of oxen or a sheepfold, and cares not though he find men and dogs keeping watch against him, so Sarpedon went against the wall. And first he spake to stout Glaucus, his comrade:—

"Tell me, Glaucus, why is it that men honour us at home with the chief rooms at feasts, and with fat portions of flesh and with sweet wine, and that we have a great domain of orchard and plough land by the banks of Xanthus? Surely it is that we may fight in the front rank.

Then shall some one who may behold us say, 'Of a truth these are honourable men, these princes of Lycia, and not without good right do they eat the fat and drink the sweet, for they fight ever in the front.' Now, indeed, if we might live forever, nor know old age nor death, neither would I fight among the first, nor would I bid thee arm thyself for the battle. But seeing that there are ten thousand fates about us which no man may avoid, let us see whether we shall win glory from another, or another shall take it from us."

And Glaucus listened to his words and charged at his side, and the great host of the Lycians followed them. Sore dismayed was Menestheus the Athenian when he saw them. All along the wall of the Greeks he looked, spying out for help; and he saw Ajax the Greater and Ajax the Less, and with them Teucer, who had just come forth from his tent. Close to him they were, but it was of no avail to shout, so loud was the clash and din of arms, of shields and helmets, and the thundering at the gates, for each one of these did the men of Troy assail.

Wherefore he called to him Thoas the herald, and said: "Run, Thoas, and call Ajax hither,— both of the name, if that may be,— for the end is close upon us in this place, so mightily press on the chiefs of the Lycians, who were ever fiery fighters. But if there is trouble there also, let at the least Ajax the Greater come, and with him Teucer with his bow."

Then the herald ran and said as he had been bidden.

And Ajax Telamon spake to the son of Oïleus: "Stand thou here with Lycomedes and stay the enemy. But I will go thither, and come again when I have finished my work."

So he went, and Teucer his brother went with him, with Pandion carrying his bow. And even as they went the Lycians came up like a tempest on the wall. But Ajax slew Epicles, a comrade of Sarpedon, smiting him on the head with a mighty stone, and crushing all the bones of his head. And Teucer smote Glaucus on the shoulder and wounded him sore. Silently did Glaucus leap down from the wall, for he would not that any of the Greeks should see that he was wounded. But Sarpedon saw that he had departed, and it grieved him. Nevertheless he ceased not from the battle, but first slew Alcmaon, the son of Mestor, and next caught one of the battlements in his hands, and dragged it down. So the wall was laid open, and a way was made for the Trojans to enter. Then did both Ajax and Teucer aim at him together. And Teucer smote the strap of the shield, but harmed him not, and Ajax drove his spear through his shield and stayed him, so that he fell back a space from the battlement, yet would not cease from the fight. Loud he shouted to the Lycians, crying : —

"Men of Lycia, why do ye abate your courage? Hard is it for me, for all that my strength is great, to break down the wall with my own hands only, and to clear the road to the ships."

So spake Sarpedon, and his people shrank from the reproach, and crowded close about their King. And on the other hand the Greeks strengthened their ranks within the wall, for the matter was of life or death. Long time they fought with equal might, for neither could the Lycians break through the wall of the Greeks and make a way to the ships, nor could the Greeks drive back the Lycians from the wall. Even as two neighbours, standing with measures in their hands, contend about some boundary, so the Lycians and the Greeks contended for the battlements. And many a man was wounded with the pitiless bronze, either smitten in the back, where he was without defence, or smitten in front through his shield; and all the battlements were bespattered with the blood of men. And still they held the scales of battle level between them, as when a just-dealing woman puts the weight in one scale and the wool in the other, and lifts them up and balances them, earning a petty gain, that she may feed her children therewith.

So it was till Zeus gave the glory to Hector. He leaped within the wall, and cried to the men of Troy, "Now follow me, and break down the wall, and burn the ships."

So he spake, and they heard his voice, and rushed together on the wall. Now in front of the gate there lay a great stone, broad at the base and sharp at the top. Scarce could two men of the strongest, such as are men in these days, move it with levers on to a wagon; but Hector lifted it easily, easily as a shepherd carries in one hand the fleece of a sheep. Two folding doors there were in the gates, held by bolts and a key, and at these he hurled the great stone, planting his feet apart, that his aim might be the surer and stronger. With a mighty crash it came against the gates, and the bolts held not against it, and the hinges were broken, so that the folding doors flew back. Then Hector leapt into the space, holding a spear in either hand, and his eyes flashed as fire. And the men of Troy came after him, some mounting the wall, and some pouring through the gates.

# CHAPTER XVI.

## THE BATTLE AT THE SHIPS.

AND when Zeus had brought the Trojans near to the ships, he turned away his eyes, and looked upon them no more, for he deemed that none of the immortal gods would come to help or Trojan or Greek. But Poseidon was watching the battle from the wooded height of Samothrace, whence he could see Ida and Troy and the ships. And he pitied the Greeks, when he saw how they fled before Hector, and purposed in his heart to help them. So he left the height of Samothrace, and came with four strides to Ægæ, where his palace was in the depths of the sea. There he harnessed the horses to his chariot, and rode, passing over the waves, and the great beasts of the sea gambolled about him as he went, knowing their king.

His horses he stabled in a cavern of the sea, and loosed them from the car, and gave them immortal food to eat, and put shackles of gold about their feet that they might abide his coming.

And all the while the men of Troy came on, following Hector, like a storm or a great flame, for they thought to take the ships and to slay the Greeks beside them.

But Poseidon came to the camp of the Greeks, taking upon him the shape of Calchas the herald. First he spake to either Ajax, saying: "Hold fast, ye men of might, so that ye save the people. For the rest of the wall I fear not, but only for the place where Hector rages. Now may some god inspire you to stand fast and drive him back."

And as he spake, he smote each with his staff, and filled them with courage, and gave strength to hands and feet. Then he passed from them even as a hawk that riseth from a cliff, chasing a bird.

And the Lesser Ajax knew him, and spake to his comrade, saying: "This is some god that bids us fight for the ships; he was not Calchas, for I marked the goings of his legs and his feet as he went. The gods are easily discerned. And verily my heart within me is eager for the fight."

The Greater Ajax answered him, " Even so do my own hands yearn about the spear, and my heart is on fire, and my feet carry me away, and I am eager to fight with Hector, even I alone, for all his fury."

Then Poseidon went to the other chiefs, going up and down the ranks, and urged them to stand fast against their enemies. But not the less did the men of Troy press on, Hector leading the way.

Among the foremost came Deïphobus, high in heart, holding his shield before him. At him Meriones cast his spear, and missed not his aim, for the spear struck full the bull's-hide shield. Yet it pierced it not, but brake; and Deïphobus held it from him, fearing greatly the stroke; but Meriones went back to his own people vexed in heart, and ran to his tent, that he might fetch another spear.

Next Teucer slew a Trojan, Imbrius by name, wounding him under the ear. He fell as some tall poplar falls which a woodman fells with axe of bronze. Then Teucer rushed to seize his arms, but Hector cast his spear. Teucer it struck not, missing him by a little;

but Amphimachus it smote on the breast so that he fell dead. Then Hector seized the dead man's helmet, seeking to drag the body among the sons of Troy. But Ajax stretched forth his great spear against him, and struck the boss of his shield mightily, driving him backwards, so that he loosed hold of the helmet of Amphimachus. And him his comrades bore to the rear of the host, and the body of Imbrius also they carried off. Then did Idomeneus the Cretan, son of Minos, the wise judge, perform many valiant deeds, going to the left-hand of the battle-line, for he said:—

"The Greeks have stay enough where the great Ajax is. No man that eats bread is better than he; no, not Achilles' self, were the two to stand man to man, but Achilles, indeed, is swifter of foot."

And first of all he slew Othryoneus, who had but newly come, hearing the fame of the war. For Cassandra's sake he had come, that he might have her to wife, vowing that he would drive the Greeks from Troy, and Priam had promised him the maiden. But now Idomeneus slew him, and cried over him:—

"This was a great thing that thou didst promise to Priam, for which he was to give thee his daughter. Thou shouldst have come to us, and we would have given thee the fairest of the daughters of Agamemnon, bringing her from Argos, if thou wouldst have engaged to help us to take this city of Troy. But come now with me to the ships, that we may treat about this marriage; thou wilt find that we have open hands."

So he spake, mocking the dead. Then King Asius charged, coming on foot with his chariot behind him. But ere he could throw his spear, Idomeneus smote him that he fell, as falls an oak, or an alder, or a pine, which men fell upon the hills. And the driver of his chariot stood dismayed, nor thought to turn his horses and flee, so that Antilochus, the son of Nestor, struck him down, and took the chariot and horses for his own. Then Deïphobus in great wrath came near to Idomeneus, and would have slain him with a spear, but could not, for he covered himself with his shield, and the spear passed over his head. Yet did it not fly in vain, for it lighted on

Hypsenor, striking him on the right side. And as he fell, Deïphobus cried aloud: —

"Now is Asius avenged; and though he go down to that strong porter who keeps the gates of hell, yet will he be glad, for I have sent him a companion."

But scarce had he spoken when Idomeneus the Cretan slew another of the chiefs of Troy, Alcathoüs, son-in-law of old Anchises. For Poseidon dazed his eyes, and spread a numbness through his limbs; he could not flee, nor yet shun the spear, but stood as stands a tree, or a stone that is a monument of the dead. Right in the breast did Idomeneus smite him, and rent the coat of bronze that shielded him from death. With a loud clash he fell, and the slayer cried: —

"Small reason hast thou to boast, Deïphobus, for we have slain three for one. But come thou and meet me in battle, that thou mayest know me who I am, son of Deucalion, who was the son of Minos, who was the son of Zeus."

Then Deïphobus thought within himself, should he meet this man alone, or should he take some brave comrade with him? And it seemed to him better that he should take a brave comrade with him. Wherefore he went for Æneas, and found him in the rear of the battle, vexed at heart because King Priam did not honour him among the princes of Troy. Then said he : —

"Come hither, Æneas, to fight for Alcathoüs, who was wont to care for thee when thou wast young, and now he lies dead under the spear of Idomeneus."

So they two went together; and Idomeneus saw them, but yielded not from his place, only called to his comrades that they should gather themselves together and help him. And on the other side Æneas called to Deïphobus, and Paris, and Agenor. So they fought about the body of Alcathoüs. Then did Æneas cast his spear at Idomeneus, but struck him not; but Idomeneus slew Œnomaüs, only when he would have spoiled him of his arms he could not, for the men of Troy pressed him hard, so that perforce he gave way. And as he turned, Deïphobus sought to slay him with his spear, but smote in his stead Ascalaphus, son of Ares. But the god, his father, knew not of it, for he sat on Olympus, kept back from the battle by the will of Zeus. Great was the fight about the dead man and his arms, for Deïphobus snatched away the helmet, but Meriones leapt forward, and struck him through the wrist with a spear. Straightway he dropped the helmet which he had seized, and Polites, his brother, led him out of the battle. And he climbed into his chariot and went back to the city. Then Peisander came against King Menelaüs; but it was an evil fate that brought him. First the son of Atreus cast his spear, but missed his aim. Then Peisander cast his spear against the shield of the King, but he could not pierce it, and the spear-head was broken off. Next the son of Atreus drew his silver-studded sword, and sprang on Peisander; and he drew from beneath his shield a goodly axe of bronze, set on a handle of olive wood. He struck the helmet of the King, beside the plume; but Menelaüs struck him in the face above the nose, and laid him dead upon the ground.

Then Menelaüs set his foot upon his breast, and spake: " Thus shall ye have the ships, ye haughty men of Troy. Ye never want for wickedness and shameful deeds. My wedded wife ye took from me, and much wealth besides; and now ye seek to burn our ships. Can it be, Father Zeus, that art the wisest of gods and men, that these things are from thee?"

Then Harpalion, son of Pylæmenes, the Paphlagonian King, leapt upon him, and smote his shield with his spear, but pierced it not. Then he fell back, avoiding death, but Meriones struck him with an arrow through the hip, and he fell, wounded to the death, and his friends lifted him upon his chariot, and bare him back to Troy.

Very wroth was Paris; for he loved Harpalion more than all the men of his land. Now there was among the Greeks one Euchenor, son of a seer of Corinth. He had come to Troy, knowing well his fate; for his father had told him that either he should perish of sickness in his hall, or be slain by the Trojans by the ships; so now Paris slew him with an arrow.

Thus on the left the Greeks beat back the men of Troy; but Hector knew not of it where he fought upon the right, pressing hard the Greeks, for there the wall was lowest, and the approach most easy. Yet there also did the defenders of the walls make a brave stand; for in the front around the Greater and the Lesser Ajax stood many mighty chiefs; and behind, the Locrians shot with their arrows. These had neither shield, nor spear, nor helmet; and it was not their custom to mingle in the press of battle. They came to Troy, trusting in their bows and slings of twisted wool, and with these they made havoc among the ranks of Troy, the warriors clad in bronze standing before and sheltering them.

Then had the men of Troy fallen back from the ships in grievous disarray, but Polydamas said to Hector: —

"O Hector, thou art ever loath to hear counsel from others. Yet think not that because thou art stronger than other men, therefore Zeus hath also made thee wiser. For truly he gives diverse gifts to diverse men — strength to one and counsel to another. Hear, then, my words. Thou seest that the Trojans keep not all together, for some stand aloof, while some fight, being few against many. Do thou therefore call the bravest together. Then shall we see whether we shall burn the ships, or, it may be, win our way back without harm to Troy; for indeed I forget not that there is a warrior here whom no man may match, nor will he, I trow, always keep aloof from the battle."

And the saying pleased Hector. So he went through the host looking for the chiefs —for Deïphobus, and Helenus, and Asius, and Acamas, son of Asius, and others, who were the bravest among the Trojans and allies. And some he found, and some he found not, for they had fallen in the battle, or had gone sorely wounded to the city. But at last he spied Paris, where he stood strengthening the hearts of his comrades. To him he spake, saying : —

"O Paris, fair of face, cheater of the hearts of women, where is Deïphobus, and Helenus, and Asius, and Acamas, son of Asius?"

But Paris answered him, "Some of these are dead, and some are sorely wounded. But we who are left fight on. Only do thou lead us against the Greeks, nor wilt thou say that we are slow to follow."

So Hector went along the front of the battle, leading the men of Troy. Nor did the Greeks give way when they saw him, but Ajax the Greater cried: —

"Friend, come near, nor fear the men of Greece. Thou thinkest in thine heart to spoil the ships, but we have hands to keep them, and ere they perish Troy itself shall fall before us. Soon, I trow, wilt thou wish that thy horses were swifter than hawks, when they bear thee fleeing before us across the plain to the city."

But Hector answered: "Nay, thou braggart Ajax, what words are these? I would that I were as surely one of the Immortals as this day shall surely bring woe to the Greeks. And thou, if thou darest to meet my spear, shalt be slain among the rest, and feed with thy flesh the beasts of the field and the fowls of the air."

So he spake, and from this side and from that there went up a great cry of battle.

# CHAPTER XVII.

### THE BATTLE AT THE SHIPS (*continued*).

So loud was the cry that it roused old Nestor where he sat in his tent, tending the wounded Machaon. Whereupon he said, " Sit thou here and drink the red wine till the fair Hecamedé shall have got ready the bath to wash the blood from thy wound ; but I will ask how things fare in the battle."

So he went forth from the tent, seeking King Agamemnon. And as he went, the King met him, and with him were Diomed and Ulysses, who also had been wounded that day. So they held counsel together. And Agamemnon — for it troubled him sore that the people were slain — would that they should draw down the ships into the sea, and should flee homewards, as soon as the darkness should cover them and the Trojans should cease from the battle.

But Ulysses would have none of such counsel, saying : " Now surely, son of Atreus, thou art not worthy to rule over us, who have been men of war from our youth. Wilt thou leave this city, for the taking of which we have suffered so much ? That may not be; let not any one of the Greeks hear thee say such words. And what is this, that thou wouldst have us launch our ships now, whilst the hosts are fighting? Surely, so doing, we should perish together, for the Greeks would not fight any more, seeing that the ships were being launched, and the men of Troy would slay us altogether."

Then King Agamemnon said, " Thou speakest well." And he went through the host, bidding the men bear themselves bravely ; and all the while Poseidon put courage and strength into their hearts ; and, on the other hand, Hera lulled Zeus to sleep on the heights of Olympus, so that now the battle went against the men of Troy. Then Hector cast his spear against Ajax Telamon. The shield kept it not off, for it passed beneath, but the two belts, of the shield and of the sword, stayed it, so that it wounded not his body. Then Hector in wrath

and fear went back into the ranks of his comrades; but as he went Ajax took a great stone
— now were there many such which they had
as props for the ships — and smote him above
the rim of his shield, on the neck.    As an oak
falls, stricken by the thunder of Zeus, so he
fell, and the Greeks rushed with a great cry to
drag him to them, but could not, for all the
bravest of the sons of Troy held their shields
before him, — Polydamas, and Æneas, and Sarpedon, and Glaucus.    Then they carried him
to the Xanthus, and poured water upon him.
And after a while he sat up, and then again
his spirit left him, for the blow had been very
grievous.    But when the Greeks saw that Hector had been carried out of the battle, they
pressed on the more, slaying the men of Troy,
and driving them back even out of the camp
and across the trench.    But when they came
to their chariots, where they had left them on
the other side of the trench, there they stood
trembling and pale with fear, as men that flee
in the day of battle.

And now Zeus woke from his sleep, and he
looked upon the earth; and he saw how the

Greeks were driving the men of Troy before them, and Hector lay upon the plain, and vomited blood, and his friends knelt about him. Senseless he lay, for it was no puny hand that had dealt the blow. Very wroth was Zeus to see such a sight, and he said to Hera: "What is this that thou hast done, sending Hector from the battle? Rememberest thou not how I hung thee amid the clouds with a band of gold about thy hands and an anvil of gold on either foot, and how when any god came to help thee I flung him from Olympus to fall till he came utterly spent to the earth? Make an end of thy deceits, or verily nothing shall protect thee from my wrath."

Then Hera answered: " It is Poseidon that afflicts the Trojans, and bears up the Greeks. Yet he, too, would do well to walk in the paths wherein thou walkest."

Then said Zeus: "Call hither Iris and Apollo the Archer; let Iris go to Poseidon, and bid him cease from the battle and get him to his own domain, and let Apollo strengthen Hector, that he may go back to the battle; so shall my will be accomplished, fulfilling the oath that I sware to Thetis of the sea that I would do honour to her son."

So he spake, and Hera obeyed his voice. To the council of the gods she went. Her brows were black with anger as she spake: "Fools! in your madness ye are wroth with Zeus, but he sitteth apart, and careth not. Take, therefore, what evil he may send, even as Ares must take the death of his son Ascalaphus, who even now hath been slain in the battle."

Then Ares started up in wrath, and smote his thighs, and said, "Nay, but I will go to the ships to avenge my son, even though I be smitten with the thunderbolt of Zeus."

So he bade Flight and Fear yoke his horses, and he donned his glittering arms. Then had the anger of Zeus fallen on the gods; but Athené rose from her seat, and caught Ares, and took the helmet from his head, and the shield from his shoulders, and the spear from his hand. "What wilt thou do, madman?" she said. "Wilt thou bring the anger of Zeus upon us all? Lay aside thy wrath for thy son, for mightier men than he have fallen."

So speaking she set Ares again in his seat.

Then Iris went to Poseidon, and gave him the message of Zeus. Very wroth was the god, and said: "Thinketh he then to control me by force who am his equal in honour? Three brethren are we, and the Fates gave the sea to me for my dominion, and to Hades the realm of darkness, and to Zeus the heaven; but the earth is for all. I walk not by the will of Zeus; let him remain in his own possessions, and meddle not."

But Iris answered: "Shaker of the earth, shall I bear back so rough an answer to Zeus? Surely thou knowest the might of the elder born?"

Then Poseidon said, "Iris, thou speakest well; this time will I yield, but know that if he shall scorn me and the other gods and let Troy stand untaken, and give not victory to the Greeks, there shall be endless feud between him and me."

Meanwhile Apollo went, at the bidding of Zeus, to Hector. He found him sitting up, for the will of Zeus had revived him. Then spake Apollo: "Hector, why sittest thou apart from thy fellows? Hath trouble come upon thee?"

Hector made reply in a feeble voice: "Who art thou among the gods that speakest to me? Knowest thou not that Ajax smote me with a mighty stone and stayed me from the battle? Verily I thought that I had gone down this day to the dwellings of the dead."

But Apollo said: "Be of good cheer, for Zeus hath sent me, who am Apollo of the Golden Sword, to stand by thee and to succour thee. Come, now, and bid thy people advance toward the ships, and I will go before thee, and make the way easy for thy horses."

So Hector rose up in his might, and entered into the battle, even as men that chase a stag or a wild goat, and lo! a lion crosseth their path, so were the Greeks afraid when they saw Hector, the son of Priam. And Thoas the Ætolian spake, saying:—

"Surely this is a great marvel that I see with mine eyes. For we thought that Hector had been slain by the hand of Ajax, son of Telamon, and now, behold! he is come back to the battle. Many Greeks have fallen before him, and many, methinks, will fall, for of a truth some god has raised him up and helps him. But come, let all the bravest stand together. So, mighty though he be, he shall fear to enter our array."

And all the bravest gathered together and stood in the front, but the multitude made for the ships. But Hector came on, and Apollo before him, with his shoulders wrapped in cloud, and the ægis shield in his hand. And many of the Greeks fell slain before the sons of Troy, as Iäsus of Athens, and Arcesilaüs the Bœotian, and Medon, who was brother to Ajax the Less, and many more. Thus the battle turned again, and came near to the trench; and now Apollo made it easy for the men of Troy to pass, so that they left not their chariots, as before, upon the brink, but drave them across.

Meanwhile Patroclus sat in the tent of Eurypylus, dressing his wound and talking with him. But when he saw what had chanced, he struck his thigh with his hand and cried: —

" Now must I leave thee, Eurypylus; for I must haste to Achilles, so dreadful is now the battle. Perchance I may persuade him that he go forth to the fight."

So he ran to the tent of Achilles. Now, indeed, the men of Troy were at the ships; for Hector and Ajax were fighting for one of them, and Ajax could not drive him back, and Hector could not burn the ship with fire. Then sprang forward Caletor with a torch in his hand, and Ajax smote him on the heart with a sword, so that he fell close by the ship. Then Hector cried:—

"Come, now, Trojans and allies, and fight for Caletor, that the Greeks spoil him not of his arms."

So saying, he cast his spear at Ajax. Him he struck not, but Cytherius, his comrade, he slew. Then was Ajax sore dismayed, and spake to Teucer, his brother:—

"See, now, Cytherius, our dear comrade, is dead, slain by Hector. But where are thy arrows and thy bow?"

So Teucer took his bow and laid an arrow on the string, and smote Clitus, who was charioteer to Polydamas. And then he aimed an arrow at Hector's self; but ere he could loose it, the bow-string was broken in his hands, and the arrow went far astray, for Zeus would not that Hector should so fall. Then Teucer cried aloud to his brother: —

"Surely some god confounds our counsels, breaking my bow-string, which this very day I tied new upon my bow."

But Ajax said: "Let be thy bow, if it please not the gods, but take spear and shield, and fight with the men of Troy. For though they master us to-day, they shall not take our ships for naught."

So Teucer armed himself afresh for the battle. But Hector, when he saw the broken bow, cried out: —

"Come on, ye men of Troy, for Zeus is with us. Even now he brake the bow of Teucer, the great archer. And they whom Zeus helps prevail, and they whom he favours not grow weak. Come on; for even though a man fall, it is well that he fall fighting for his fatherland; and his wife and his children are safe, nor shall his glory cease, if so be that we drive the Greeks in their ships across the sea."

And on the other side Ajax, the son of Telamon, called to the Greeks and bade them quit themselves like men. Then the battle grew yet fiercer, for Hector slew Schedius, who led the men of Phocis, and Ajax slew Laodamas, son of Antenor, and Polydamas Otus of Cyllene. Then Meges thought to slay Polydamas; but his spear went astray, smiting down Cræsmus; and Dolops, who was grandson to Laomedon, cast his spear at Meges, but the corselet stayed the point, though it pierced the shield. But Dolops' self Menelaüs smote through the shoulder, but could not spoil him of his arms, for Hector and his brothers hindered him. So they fought, slaying one another; but Hector still waxed greater and greater in the battle, and still the men of Troy came on, and still the Greeks gave way. So they came again, these pushing forward and these yielding ground, to the ships. And Hector caught hold of one of them, even the ship of Protesilaüs: him, indeed, it had brought from Troy, but it took him not back, for he had fallen, slain by the hand of Hector, as he leapt, first of all the Greeks, upon the shore of Troy. This Hector caught, and the battle raged like

Ajax defending the Greek Ships against the Trojans.

fire about it; for the men of Troy and the Greeks were gathered round, and none fought with arrows or javelins from afar, but man to man, with battle-axe and sword and great spears pointed at either end. And many a fair weapon lay shattered on the ground, and the earth flowed with blood as with a river. But still Hector held the stem of the ship with his hand, and called to the men of Troy that they should bring fire, for that Zeus had given them the victory that day. Then even Ajax himself gave way, so did the spears of the Trojans press him; for now he stood no longer upon the stern deck, but on the rowers' bench, thrusting thence with his spear at any one who sought to set fire to the ship. And ever he cried to the Greeks with a terrible voice:—

"O ye Greeks! now must ye quit yourselves like men. For have ye any helpers behind? or have ye any walls to shelter you? No city is here, with well-built battlements, wherein ye might be safe, while the people should fight for you. For we are here in the plain of Troy, and the sea is close behind us, and we are far from our country. Wherefore all our hope is in valour, and not in shrinking back from the battle."

And still he thrust with his spear, if any of the men of Troy, at Hector's bidding, sought to bring fire against the ships. Full twelve he wounded where he stood.

# CHAPTER XVIII.

## THE DEEDS AND DEATH OF PATROCLUS.

PATROCLUS stood by Achilles, weeping bitterly. Then said Achilles: "What ails thee, Patroclus, that thou weepest like a girl-child that runs along by her mother's side, and would be taken up, holding her gown, and looking at her with tearful eyes till she lift her in her arms? Hast thou heard evil news from Phthia? Menœtius yet lives, they say, and Peleus. Or art thou weeping for the Greeks, because they perish for their folly?"

Then said Patroclus: "Be not wroth with me, great Achilles, for indeed the Greeks are in grievous straits, and all their bravest are wounded, and still thou cherishest thy wrath. Surely Peleus was not thy father, nor Thetis thy mother; but the rocks begat thee, and the sea brought thee forth. Or if thou goest not to the battle, fearing some warning from the gods, yet let me go, and thy Myrmidons with me. And let me put thy armour on me; so shall the Greeks have breathing-space from the war."

So he spake, entreating, nor knew that for his own doom he entreated. And Achilles made reply: —

"It is no warning that I heed, that I keep back from the war. But these men took from me my prize, which I won with my own hands. But let the past be past. I said that I would not rise up till the battle should come nigh to my own ships. But thou mayest put my armour upon thee, and lead my Myrmidons to the fight. For in truth the men of Troy are gathered as a dark cloud about the ships, and the Greeks have scarce standing-ground between them and the sea. For they see not the gleam of my helmet. And Diomed is not there with his spear; nor do I hear the voice of Agamemnon, but only the voice of Hector, as he calls the men of Troy to the battle. Go, therefore, Patroclus, and drive the fire from the ships. And then come thou back, nor fight any more with the Trojans, lest thou take my glory from me. And go not near, in the delight of battle, to the walls of Troy, lest one of the gods meet thee to thy hurt; and, of a truth, the keen archer Apollo loves the Trojans well."

But as they talked the one to the other, Ajax could hold out no longer. For swords and javelins came thick upon him, and clattered on his helmet, and his shoulder was weary with the great shield which he held; and he breathed heavily and hard, and the great drops of sweat fell upon the ground. Then at the last Hector came near and smote his spear with a great sword, so that the head fell off. Then was Ajax sore afraid, and gave way, and the men of Troy set torches to the ship's stem, and a great flame shot up to the sky. And Achilles saw it, and smote his thigh and spake: —

"Haste thee, Patroclus, for I see the fire rising up from the ships. Put thou on the armour, and I will call my people to the war."

So Patroclus put on the armour, — corselet, and shield, and helmet, — and bound upon his shoulder the silver-studded sword, and took a mighty spear in his hand. But the great Pelian spear he took not, for that no man but

Achilles might wield. Then Automedon yoked the horses to the chariot, Bayard and Piebald, and with them in the side harness, Pedasus; and they two were deathless steeds, but he was mortal.

Meanwhile Achilles had called the Myrmidons to battle. Fifty ships had he brought to Troy, and in each there were fifty men. Five leaders they had, and the bravest of the five was Pisander.

Then Achilles said: " Forget not, ye Myrmidons, the bold words that ye spake against the men of Troy during the days of my wrath, making complaint that I kept you from the battle against your will. Now, therefore, ye have that which you desired."

So the Myrmidons went to the battle in close array, helmet to helmet and shield to shield, close as the stones with which a builder builds a wall. And in front went Patroclus, and Automedon in the chariot beside him. Then Achilles went to his tent and took a great cup from the chest, which Thetis his mother had given him. Now no man drank of that cup but he only, nor did he pour out of it libations to any of the gods, but only to Zeus. This first he cleansed with sulphur, and then with water from the spring. And after this he washed his hands, and stood in the midst of the space before his tent, and poured out of it to Zeus, saying, " O Zeus, I send my comrade to this battle; make him strong and bold, and give him glory, and bring him home safe to the ships, and my people with him."

So he prayed, and Father Zeus heard him, and part he granted and part denied.

But now Patroclus with the Myrmidons had come to where the battle was raging about the ship of Protesilaüs, and when the men of Troy beheld him, they thought that Achilles had forgotten his wrath and was come forth to the war. And first Patroclus slew Pyræchmes, who was the chief of the Pæonians who live on the banks of the broad Axius. Then the men of Troy turned to flee, and many chiefs of fame fell by the spears of the Greeks. So the battle rolled back to the trench, and in the trench many chariots of the Trojans were broken, but the horses of Achilles went across it at a stride, so nimble were they and strong.

And the heart of Patroclus was set to slay Hector; but he could not overtake him, so swift were his horses. Then did Patroclus turn his chariot, and keep back those that fled, that they should not go to the city, and rushed hither and thither, still slaying as he went.

But Sarpedon, when he saw the Lycians dismayed and scattered, called to them that they should be of good courage, saying that he would himself make trial of this great warrior. So he leapt down from his chariot, and Patroclus also leapt down, and they rushed at each other as two eagles rush together. Then first Patroclus struck down Thrasymelus, who was the comrade of Sarpedon; and Sarpedon, who had a spear in either hand, with the one struck the horse Pedasus, which was of mortal breed, on the right shoulder, and with the other missed his aim, sending it over the left shoulder of Patroclus. But Patroclus missed not his aim, driving his spear into Sarpedon's heart. Then fell the great Lycian chief, as an oak, or a poplar, or a pine falls upon the hills before the axe. But he called to Glaucus, his companion, saying: "Now must thou show thyself a good warrior, Glaucus. First call the men of Lycia to fight for me, and do thou fight thyself, for it would be foul shame to thee, all thy days, if the Greeks should spoil me of my arms."

Then he died. But Glaucus was sore troubled, for he could not help him, so grievous was the wound where Teucer had wounded him. Therefore he prayed to Apollo, and Apollo helped him and made him whole. Then he went first to the Lycians, bidding them fight for their King, and then to the chiefs of the Trojans, that they should save the body of Sarpedon. And to Hector he said: " Little carest thou for thy allies. Lo! Sarpedon is dead, slain by Patroclus. Suffer not the Myrmidons to carry him off and do dishonour to his body."

But Hector was troubled to hear such news, and so were all the sons of Troy, for Sarpedon was the bravest of the allies, and led most people to the battle. So with a great shout they charged, and drove the Greeks back a space from the body; and then again the Greeks did the like. And so the battle raged, till no one would have known the great Sarpedon, so covered was he with spears and blood and dust. But at the last the Greeks drave back the men of Troy from the body, and stripped the arms, but the body itself they harmed not. For Apollo came down at the bidding of Zeus and carried it out of the midst of the battle, and washed it with water, and anointed it with ambrosia, and wrapped it in garments of the gods. And then he gave it to Sleep and Death, and these two carried it to Lycia, his fatherland.

Then did Patroclus forget the word which Achilles had spoken to him, that he should not go near to Troy, for he pursued the men of the city even to the wall. Thrice he mounted on the angle of the wall, and thrice Apollo himself drove him back, pushing his shining shield. But the fourth time the god said : " Go thou back, Patroclus. It is not for thee to take the city of Troy; no, nor for Achilles, who is far better than thou art."

So Patroclus went back, fearing the wrath of the archer god. Then Apollo stirred up the spirit of Hector, that he should go against

Sleep and Death conveying the Body of Sarpedon to Lycia.

Patroclus. Therefore he went, with his brother Cebriones for driver of his chariot. But when they came near, Patroclus cast a great stone which he had in his hand, and smote Cebriones on the forehead, crushing it in, so that he fell headlong from the chariot. And Patroclus mocked him, saying:—

"How nimble is this man! how lightly he dives! What spoil he would take of oysters, diving from a ship, even in a stormy sea! Who would have thought that there were such skilful divers in Troy!"

Then again the battle waxed hot about the body of Cebriones, and this too, at the last, the Greeks drew unto themselves, and spoiled it of the arms. And this being accomplished, Patroclus rushed against the men of Troy. Thrice he rushed, and each time he slew nine chiefs of fame. But the fourth time Apollo stood behind him and struck him on the head and shoulders, so that his eyes were darkened. And the helmet fell from off his head, so that the horse-hair plumes were soiled with dust. Never before had it touched the ground, for it was the helmet of Achilles. And also the god brake the spear in his hand, and struck the shield from his arms, and loosed his corselet. All amazed he stood, and then Euphorbus, son of Panthoüs, smote him on the back with his spear, but slew him not. Then Patroclus sought to flee to the ranks of his comrades. But Hector saw him, and thrust at him with his spear, smiting him in the groin, so that he fell. And when the Greeks saw him fall, they sent up a terrible cry. Then Hector stood over him and cried:—

"Didst thou think to spoil our city, Patroclus, and to carry away our wives and daughters in the ships? But lo! I have slain thee, and the fowls of the air shall eat thy flesh; nor shall the great Achilles help thee at all— Achilles, who bade thee, I trow, strip the tunic from my breast, and thou thoughtest in thy folly to do it."

But Patroclus answered: "Thou boasteth much, Hector. Yet *thou* didst not slay me, but Apollo, who took from me my arms, for had twenty such as thou met me, I had slain them all. And mark thou this: death and fate are close to thee by the hand of the great Achilles."

And Hector answered, but Patroclus was dead already: "Why dost thou prophesy death to me? May be the great Achilles himself shall fall by my hand."

Then he drew his spear from the wound, and went after Automedon, to slay him, but the swift horses of Achilles carried him away.

# CHAPTER XIX.

## THE ROUSING OF ACHILLES.

FIERCE was the fight about the body of Patroclus, and many heroes fell, both on this side and on that, and first of them all Euphorbus, who first had wounded him. For as he came near to strip the dead man of his arms, Menelaüs slew him with his spear. He slew him, but took not his arms, for Hector came through the battle; nor did Menelaüs dare to abide his coming, but went back into the ranks of his own people. Then did Hector strip off the arms of Patroclus, the arms which the great Achilles had given him to wear. Then he laid hold of the body, and would have dragged it into the host of the Trojans, but Ajax Telamon came forth, and put his broad shield before it, as a lion stands before its cubs when the hunters meet it in the woods, drawing down over its eyes its shaggy brows.

THE FIGHT FOR THE BODY OF PATROCLUS.

Then Hector gave place, but Glaucus saw him, and said: —

"Now is this a shame to thee, that thou darest not to stand against Ajax. How wilt thou and thy countrymen save the city of Troy? For surely no more will thy allies fight for it. Small profit have they of thee. Did not Sarpedon fall, and didst thou not leave him to be a prey to the dogs? And now, if thou hadst stood firm and carried off Patroclus, we might have made exchange, and gained from the Greeks Sarpedon and his arms. But it may not be, for thou fearest Ajax, and fleest before him."

But Hector said: "I fear him not, nor any man. Only Zeus giveth victory now to one man and now to another. But wait thou here, and see whether I be a coward, as thou sayest."

Now he had sent the armour of Patroclus to the city. But now he ran after those that were carrying it, and overtook them, and put on the armour himself (but Zeus saw him doing it, and liked it not), and came back to the battle; and all who saw him thought that it had been the great Achilles himself. Then they all charged together, and fiercer grew the battle and fiercer as the day went on. For the Greeks said one to another: "Now had the earth better yawn and swallow us up alive, than we should let the men of Troy carry off Patroclus to their city"; and the Trojans said: "Now if we must all fall by the body of this man, be it so, but we will not yield." But the horses of Achilles stood apart from the battle, when they knew that Patroclus was dead, and wept. Nor could Automedon move them with the lash, nor with gentle words, nor with threats. They would not return to the ships, nor would they go into the battle; but as a pillar stands on the tomb of some dead man, so they stood, with their heads drooped to the ground, and with big tears dropping to the earth, and their long manes trailing in the dust.

But Father Zeus beheld them, and pitied them, and said: —

"It was not well that we gave you, immortal as ye are, to a mortal man; for of all things that move on earth, mortal man is the fullest of sorrow. But Hector shall not possess you.

It is enough for him, yea, and too much, that he hath the arms of Achilles."

Then did the horses move from their place, and obey their charioteer as before. Nor could Hector take them, though he desired them very much. And all the while the battle raged about the dead Patroclus. And at last Ajax said to Menelaüs (now these two had borne themselves more bravely in the fight than all others) : —

"See if thou canst find Antilochus, Nestor's son, that he may carry the tidings to Achilles, how that Patroclus is dead."

So Menelaüs went and found Antilochus on the left of the battle, and said to him : " I have ill news for thee. Thou seest that the men of Troy have the victory to-day. And also Patroclus lies dead. Run, therefore, to Achilles, and tell him, if haply he may save the body ; but as for the arms, Hector has them already."

Sore dismayed was Antilochus to hear such tidings, and his eyes were filled with tears, and his voice was choked. Yet did he give heed to the words of Menelaüs, and ran to tell Achilles of what had chanced. But Menelaüs went back to Ajax, where he had left him by Patroclus, and said:—

"Antilochus, indeed, bears the tidings to Achilles. Yet I doubt whether he will come, for all his wrath against Hector, seeing that he has no armour to cover him. Let us think, then, how we may best carry Patroclus away from the men of Troy."

Then said Ajax, "Do thou and Meriones run forward and raise the body in your arms, and I and the son of Oïleus will keep off, meanwhile, the men of Troy."

So Menelaüs and Meriones ran forward and lifted up the body. And the Trojans ran forward with a great shout when they saw them, as dogs run barking before the hunters when they chase a wild boar; but when the beast turns to bay, then they flee this way and that. So did the men of Troy flee when Ajax the Greater and Ajax the Less turned to give battle. But still the Greeks gave way, and still the Trojans came on, and ever in the front were Hector, the son of Priam, and Æneas, the son of Anchises. But in the meantime Antilochus came near to Achilles, who, indeed, seeing that the Greeks fled and the men of Troy pursued, was already sore afraid. And he said, weeping as he spake:—

"I bring ill news,— Patroclus lies low. The Greeks fight for his body, but Hector has his arms."

Then Achilles took of the dust of the plain in his hand, and poured it on his head, and lay at his length upon the ground, and tare his hair. And all the women wailed. And Antilochus sat weeping; but ever he held the hands of Achilles, lest he should slay himself in his great grief.

Then came his mother, hearing his cry, from where she sat in the depths of the sea, and laid her hand on him and said:—

"Why weepest thou, my son? Hide not the matter from me, but tell me."

And Achilles answered: "All that Zeus promised thee for me he hath fulfilled. But what profit have I, for my friend Patroclus is dead, and Hector has the arms which I gave him to wear. And as for me, I care not to live, except I can avenge me upon him."

Then said Thetis: "Nay, my son, speak not

thus. For when Hector dieth, thy doom also is near."

And Achilles spake in great wrath: "Would that I might die this hour, seeing that I could not help my friend, but am a burden on the earth — I, who am better in battle than all the Greeks besides. Cursed be the wrath that sets men to strive the one with the other, even as it set me to strive with King Agamemnon! But let the past be past. And as for my fate — let it come when it may, so that I first avenge myself on Hector. Wherefore, seek not to keep me back from the battle."

Then Thetis said: "Be it so; only thou canst not go without thy arms, which Hector hath. But to-morrow will I go to Hephæstus, that he may furnish thee anew."

But while they talked the men of Troy pressed the Greeks more and more, and the two heroes, Ajax the Greater and Ajax the Less, could no longer keep Hector back, but that he should lay hold of the body of Patroclus. And indeed he would have taken it, but that Zeus sent Iris to Achilles, who said: —

" Rouse thee, son of Peleus, or Patroclus will be a prey for the dogs of Troy!"

But Achilles said: " How shall I go?—for arms have I none, nor know I whose I might wear. Haply I could shift with the shield of Ajax, son of Telamon, but he, I know, is carrying it in the front of the battle."

Then answered Iris, "Go only to the trench and show thyself; so shall the men of Troy tremble and cease from the battle, and the Greeks shall have breathing-space."

So he went, and Athené put her ægis about his mighty shoulders, and a golden halo about his head, making it shine as a flame of fire, even as the watch-fires shine at night from some city that is besieged. Then went he to the trench; with the battle he mingled not, heeding his mother's commands, but he shouted aloud, and his voice was as the sound of a trumpet. And when the men of Troy heard, they were stricken with fear, and the horses backed with the chariots, and the drivers were astonished when they saw the flaming fire above his head which Athené had kindled. Thrice across the trench the great Achilles shouted, and thrice the men of Troy fell back.   And that hour there perished twelve chiefs of fame, wounded by their own spears or trampled by their own steeds, so great was the terror among the men of Troy.

Right gladly did the Greeks take Patroclus out of the press.  Then they laid him on a bier, and carried him to the tent, Achilles walking with many tears by his side.

But on the other side the men of Troy held an assembly.  Standing they held it, for none dared to sit, lest Achilles should be upon them.

Then spake Polydamas: "Let us not wait here for the morning.  It was well for us to fight at the ships while Achilles yet kept his wrath against Agamemnon.  But now it is not so.  For to-morrow he will come against us in his anger, and many will fall before him. Wherefore, let us go back to the city, for high are the walls and strong the gates, and he will perish before he pass them."

Then said Hector: "This is ill counsel, Polydamas.  Shall we shut ourselves up in the city, where all our goods are wasted already, buying meat for the people?  Nay, let us watch to-night, and to-morrow will we fight with the Greeks. And if Achilles be indeed come forth from his tent, be it so. I will not shun to meet him, for Ares gives the victory now to one man and now to another."

So he spake, and all the people applauded, foolish, not knowing what the morrow should bring forth.

# CHAPTER XX.

### THE MAKING OF THE ARMS.

MEANWHILE in the camp of the Greeks they mourned for Patroclus. And Achilles stood among his Myrmidons and said : —

"Vain was the promise that I made to Menœtius that I would bring back his son with his portion of the spoils of Troy. But Zeus fulfils not the thoughts of man. For he lies dead, nor shall I return to the house of Peleus, my father, for I, too, must die in this land. But thee, O Patroclus, I will not bury till I bring hither the head and the arms of Hector, and twelve men of Troy to slay at thy funeral pile."

So they washed the body of Patroclus and anointed it, putting ointment nine years old into the wounds, and laid it on a bed, and covered it with a linen cloth from the head to the feet, and laid a white robe over it. All night the Myrmidons mourned for Patroclus dead ; and Zeus spake to Hera, saying : —

" So thou hast had thy will, and hast roused Achilles, the swift of foot. Truly thou art as a mother to the Greeks ! "

And Hera answered: " Will not a man make good his word to his fellow, though he be but a man? Then how should I, who am chief among the goddesses, not send trouble on the Trojans, against whom I have great wrath ? "

But Thetis went to the house of Hephæstus. She found him busy at his work, making twenty cauldrons with three feet, that were to stand about the house of the gods. Golden wheels had they beneath, that they might go of their own motion into the chambers of the gods, and of their own motion return. But Charis, which is by interpretation Grace, that was wife to Hephæstus, espied Thetis, and caught her by the hands, and said, " Why, goddess, whom we love and honour, comest thou to our house, though thou art not wont so to do ? "

So spake she, and led her in, and set her on a silver-studded chair, and put a chair beneath her feet. Then she called to her husband, saying : —

“ Come quick.  Thetis would have somewhat of thee.”

And he said: “ Verily, there is one in my house that was my saviour in the day of trouble; for my mother cast me out because I was lame, but Thetis and her sister received me in the sea.  Nine years I dwelt with them, and hammered many a trinket in a hollow cave.  Verily, I would pay the price of my life for Thetis.”

Then he put away his tools, and washed himself, and took a staff in his hand, and came into the house, and sat upon a chair, and said: “ Speak all thy mind.  I will do thy pleasure, if it can be done.”

Then did Thetis tell him of her son Achilles, and of the wrong that had been done to him, and of his wrath, and of how Patroclus was dead, and that the arms that he had had were lost.

“ Make me now,” she said, “for him a shield and a helmet, and greaves, and a corselet.”

And Hephæstus answered: “ Be of good cheer.  Would that I could keep from him the doom of death as easily as I can make him such arms that a man will wonder when he looks upon them."

Then he went to his smithy, and turned the bellows to the fire, and bade them work. Also he put bronze and tin and gold and silver into the fire, to melt them, and set the anvil, and took the hammer in one hand, and the tongs in the other.

First he made a shield, great and strong, and fastened thereto a belt of silver. On it he wrought the earth, and the sky, and the sea, and the sun, and the moon, and all the stars. He wrought also two cities. In the one there was peace, and about the other there was war. For in the first they led a bride to her home with music and dancing, and the women stood in the doors to see the show, and in the market-place the judges judged about one that had been slain, and one man said that he had paid the price of blood, and the other denied. But about the other city there sat an army besieging it, and the men of the city stood upon the wall defending it. These had also set an ambush by a river where the herds were wont to drink. And when the herds came down,

they rose up and took them and slew the herdsmen. But the army of the besiegers heard the
cry, and came swiftly on horses, and fought by
the bank of the river. Also he wrought one
field where many men drove the plough, and
another where reapers reaped the corn, and
boys gathered it in their arms to bind into
sheaves, while the lord stood glad at heart,
beholding them. Also he wrought a vineyard,
wherein was a path, and youths and maidens
bearing baskets of grapes, and in the midst a
boy played on a harp of gold and sang a pleasant song. Also he made a herd of oxen going
from the stables to the pastures, and herdsmen
and dogs, and in the front two lions had caught
a mighty bull and were devouring it, while the
dogs stood far off and barked. Also he made
a sheepfold; also a marvellous dance of men
and maidens, and these had coronets of gold,
and those daggers of gold hanging from belts
of silver. And round about the shield he
wrought the great river of ocean.

Besides the shield, he also made a corselet
brighter than fire, and a great helmet with a
ridge of gold for the crest, and greaves of tin.

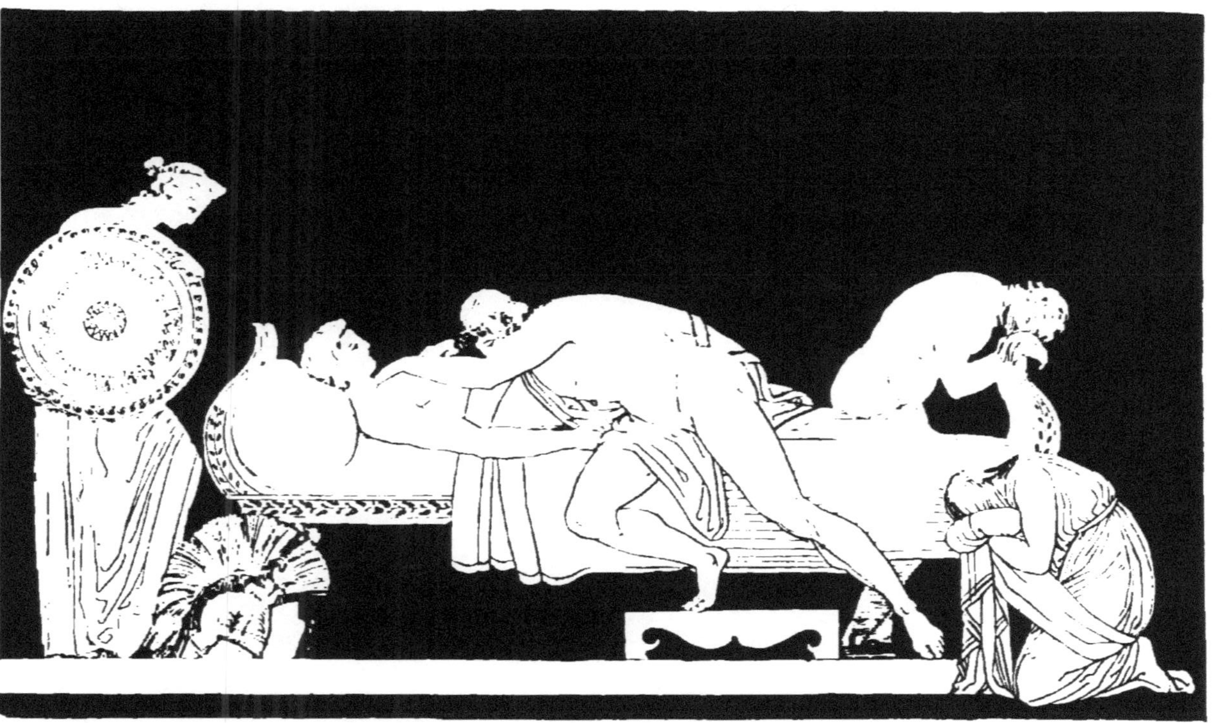

THETIS BRINGING THE ARMOUR TO ACHILLES.

And when he had finished all the armour, he set them before the mother of Achilles. Like to a hawk did she leap from Olympus, carrying them to her son. And when she came to the ships, she found him lying on the earth with his arms about the body of Patroclus, weeping aloud, and his men stood about lamenting.

The goddess stood in the midst, and clasped her son by the hand, and spake: "Come, now, let us leave the dead man; for he hath been slain according to the ordering of the gods. And do thou receive from Hephæstus this armour, exceeding beautiful, such as man never yet wore upon his shoulders."

So she spake, and cast the armour before Achilles. Loud did it rattle as it fell, and the Myrmidons feared to look upon the sight. But Achilles took the splendid armour into his hand, and was glad, and spake, saying: "Mother, the gods have given me arms, such as it is fitting should be made in heaven, and I vow I will arm me for the fight. Yet much I fear that decay will mar the body of Patroclus, now that the life hath gone from out of it."

But Thetis made answer: "Let not this

trouble thee; I will keep decay from his flesh, yea, though he should lie here till the year come round again. Go, then, and call the people to the assembly, and put away thy wrath against King Agamemnon, and arm thyself for the battle."

So she spake, putting trust and valour into his soul; and into the nostrils of the dead man she poured ambrosia and ruddy nectar, that his flesh might be sweet.

# CHAPTER XXI.

## THE ENDING OF THE STRIFE.

ACHILLES went along the shore of the sea, shouting aloud to the warriors. And at his call they came, even they who before had remained at the ships, as the pilots and they who dealt out the food, because Achilles, who had been absent so long from the battle, had returned thereto. Also Diomed and Ulysses came to the assembly, leaning on spears, for their wounds were fresh, and King Agamemnon.

Then Achilles stood up, and spake: " It was ill done, son of Atreus, that we strove for a woman! Would that Artemis had slain her with an arrow on the day when I took her captive! Many a Greek who hath now bitten the ground had then lived, and the Trojans had not reaped such profit from our wrath. But come, let the past be past. Here I make an end of my anger. And now make haste, and send the Greeks to battle.    Let us see whether the men of Troy will camp beside the ships."

Then said Agamemnon, speaking from his place: "Listen, ye Greeks.   Oft have ye blamed me for this quarrel.   Yet it was not I that was in fault; rather it was Zeus and Fate, and the Fury that walketh in darkness.   But to thee, Achilles, I make full amends, for here I offer thee the gifts which Ulysses promised thee yesterday.   Stay awhile, while my people bring them from my ships."

To him Achilles made answer:   "Give thy gifts, O King, if it be thy will, or keep them to thyself.   But let us turn without delay to the battle."

Then spake the wise Ulysses: "Achilles, urge not the Greeks to enter fasting into the battle: for verily the strife will not be short, seeing that both this host and that are inspired with might from heaven.   A man that hath not eaten cannot fight till set of sun, for his limbs grow heavy unawares, and he is hindered by hunger and thirst.   Bid, therefore, the people disperse, and make ready their food.   Meanwhile, let King Agamemnon send for the gifts and deliver them to thee in full assembly. And afterwards let him furnish a feast of reconciliation, that so thou mayest miss nothing of thy due."

Then said the King: " Thou speakest well, Ulysses. Do thou thyself fetch the gifts, and let the herald fetch us a boar, that we may do sacrifice to Zeus and to the Sun."

But Achilles said : " This business had suited better some other time, as when there was some breathing-space in the war, and my heart was not so hot within me. But now the dead whom Hector slew lieth low, and ye bid me think of food. Let the Greeks enter fasting into battle, and make them a great supper when the sun goes down. As for me, neither food nor drink shall pass my lips."

To him Ulysses made reply: " Thou art the stronger, son of Peleus, yet I may be the wiser, for I am older than thou, and of more experience. Ask not the Greeks to fast because of the dead. Verily they fall every day. How, then, should there be any interval of grief? Rather let us bury him that dieth, and bewail him for a day, and harden our hearts to forget:

and then let us who are left eat and drink, that we may fight with better heart."

Then did Ulysses go to the tent of the King; and they brought thence the gifts, seven tripods, and twenty caldrons, and twelve horses, and seven women, skilled workers with the needle, and the fair Briseïs the eighth. And before them came Ulysses, bearing the talents of gold, full weight of the balance.

These the Myrmidons took to the tent of Achilles. But when Briseïs saw Patroclus, she beat her breast and her fair face and neck, and wailed aloud, for he had been gentle and good, she said. And all the women wailed with her, thinking each of her own sorrows.

Then the chiefs would have Achilles feast with them; but he hearkened not, for he would neither eat nor drink till he had had vengeance for the dead. And he spake, saying: " Often, Patroclus, hast thou ordered the feast when we were hastening to the war. And now thou liest slain, and for grief for thee I cannot eat nor drink. For greater sorrow could not have come to me, not though Peleus himself were dead, or my young son Neoptolemus. Often did I think that I only should perish here, but that thou shouldst return and show my son all that was mine, goods and servants and palace."

And as he wept, the old men wept with him, thinking each of what he had left at home.

But Zeus said to Athené: "Carest thou not for Achilles that is so dear to thee? See, the other Greeks are gone to their meal, but he sits fasting."

Then Athené leapt down from heaven, and shed into the breast of Achilles nectar and ambrosia, that his knees should not fail from hunger.

Meanwhile the Greeks poured out to battle, and in the midst Achilles armed himself. He put the lordly greaves about his legs, and fitted the corselet on his breast. From his shoulders he hung the sword, and he took the great shield that Hephæstus had made, and it blazed as it were the heaven. Also he put the helmet on his head, and the plumes waved all around. Then he made trial of the arms, and they fitted him well, and bare him up like wings. Last he drew from its case his father's spear, which Cheiron cut on the top of Pelion, to be the death of many, and none might wield it but Achilles' self. Then he spake to his horses: "Take heed, Bayard and Piebald, that ye save your driver to-day, nor leave him dead on the field, as ye left Patroclus."

Then Hera gave to the horse Bayard a voice, so that he spake: "Surely we will save thee, great Achilles; yet for all that, doom is near to thee, nor are we the cause, but the gods and mastering Fate. Nor was it of us that Patroclus died, but Apollo slew him and gave the glory to Hector. So shalt thou, too, die by the hands of a god and of a mortal man."

And Achilles said: "What need to tell me of my doom? Right well I know it. Yet will I not cease till I have made the Trojans weary of battle."

# CHAPTER XXII.

## THE BATTLE AT THE RIVER.

THUS did Achilles go again into the battle, eager above all things to meet with Hector and to slay him.

But Apollo stood by Æneas, and spake to him, "Æneas, where are now thy boastings that thou wouldst meet Achilles face to face?"

Then Æneas answered: "Nay, I have stood up against him in the day when he took the town of Lyrnessus. But I fled before him, and only my nimble feet saved me from falling by his spear. Surely a god is ever with him, making his spear to fly aright."

Him Apollo answered again: "Thou, too, art the son of a goddess, and thy mother is greater than his, for she is but a daughter of the Sea. Drive straight at him with thy spear, and let not his threats dismay thee."

Then Æneas stood out from the press to meet Achilles, and Achilles said : " Fightest thou with me because thou hopest to reign over the men of Troy, or have they given thee a choice portion of ground, ploughland and orchard, to be thine when thou hast slain me? Thou wilt not find it easy. Dost thou not remember how thou fleddest before me in the day that I took Lyrnessus?"

Then Æneas answered: "Think not to terrify me with words, son of Peleus, for I, too, am the son of a goddess. Let us make trial one of the other."

Then he cast his spear, and it struck the shield of Achilles with so dreadful a sound that the hero feared lest it should pierce it through, knowing not that the gifts of the gods are not easy for mortal man to vanquish. Two folds, indeed, it pierced, that were of bronze, but in the gold it was stayed, and there were yet two of tin within. Then Achilles cast his spear. Through the shield of Æneas it passed, and though it wounded him not, yet was he sore dismayed, so near it came. Then Achilles drew his sword, and rushed on Æneas, and Æneas caught up a great stone to cast at him. But it was not the will of the gods that Æneas should perish, seeing that he and his sons after him should rule over the men of Troy in the ages to come. Therefore Poseidon lifted him up, and bore him over the ranks of men to the left of the battle, but first he drew the spear out of the shield, and laid it at the feet of Achilles. Much the hero marvelled to see it, crying: " This is a great wonder that I behold with mine eyes. For I see my spear before me, but the man whom I sought to slay I see not. Of a truth Æneas spake truth, saying that he was dear to the immortal gods."

Then he rushed into the battle, slaying as he went. And Hector would have met him, but Apollo stood by him, and said, " Fight not with Achilles, lest he slay thee." Therefore he went back among the men of Troy. Many did Achilles slay, and among them Polydorus, son of Priam, who, because he was the youngest and very dear, his father suffered not to go to the battle. Yet he went, in his folly, and being very swift of foot, he trusted in his speed, running through the foremost of the fighters. But as he ran, Achilles smote him, and wounded him to the death. When Hector saw it, he could not bear any more to stand apart. Therefore he rushed at Achilles, and Achilles rejoiced to see him, saying, "This is the man who slew my comrade." And to Hector he cried, "Come hither, and taste of death."

And Hector made answer: "Son of Peleus, seek not to make me afraid with words. For though I be weaker than thou, yet victory lieth on the knees of the gods, and I, too, bear a spear."

Then he cast his spear; but Athené turned it aside with her breath, and laid it again at his feet. And when Achilles leapt upon Hector with a shout, Apollo snatched him away. Three times did Achilles leap upon him, and three times he struck only the mist. But the fourth time he cried with a terrible voice, "Dog, thou hast escaped from death, Apollo helping thee; but I shall meet thee again, and make an end of thee."

Then Achilles turned to the others, and slew multitudes of them, so that they fled, some across the plain, and some to the river, the eddying Xanthus. And these leapt into the water as locusts leap into a river when a fire which men light drives them from the fields. And all the river was full of horses and men. Then Achilles leapt into the stream, leaving his spear on the bank, resting on the tamarisk trees. Only his sword had he, and with this he slew many; and they were as fishes which fly from some great dolphin in the sea. In all the bays of a harbour they hide themselves, for the great beast devours them apace. So did the Trojans hide themselves under the banks of the river. And when Achilles was weary of slaying, he took twelve alive, whom he would slay on the tomb of Patroclus.

Then met he with a son of Priam, Lycaon by name, whom he had taken captive before. He had found him in his father's vineyard, making the rims of a chariot from a wild fig-tree trunk, and sold him across the sea to Lemnos. There a friend ransomed him for a goodly price; so he came again to his father's house. For eleven days he feasted with his comrades, and on the twelfth went forth to the battle. Thus did Fate put him again into the hands of Achilles.

Then Achilles said: " This is a wonder that I see. The Trojans whom I sold across the sea come back. Now shall this man taste of my spear, and I will mark whether he shall return again from below the earth, from the place that holdeth the mighty fast."

But when he lifted his spear, Lycaon ran beneath it, and caught him by the knees, and prayed, saying, " Slay me not, I beseech thee, but take ransom for my life, for though I be Priam's son, I am not own brother to Hector that slew thy friend."

But Achilles would have no pity, but slew him, and taking the body by the foot, cast it into the river, saying, " Lie there and feed the fishes; no mother shall lay thee on a bed, and make lamentation over thee."

Then next there met him Asteropæus, who was the grandson of the river-god Axius, and led the men of Pæonia. And Achilles wondered to see him, and said, " Who art thou, that standest against me ? "

And he said, " I am the grandson of the

river-god Axius, fairest of all the streams on the earth, and I lead the men of Pæonia."

And as he spake he cast two spears, one with each hand, for he could use either alike; and the one struck the shield, nor pierced it through, for the gold stayed it, and the other grazed the right hand so that the blood spurted forth. Then did Achilles cast his spear, but missed his aim, and the great spear stood fast in the bank. And thrice Asteropæus strove to draw it forth. Thrice he strove in vain, and the fourth time he strove to break the spear. But as he strove Achilles smote him that he died. Yet had he some glory, for that he wounded the great Achilles.

# CHAPTER XXIII.

### THE BATTLE OF THE GODS.

WHEN the River saw that Asteropæus was dead, and that Achilles was slaying many of the Pæonians — for these were troubled, their chief being dead — he took upon him the shape of a man, and spake to Achilles, saying: " Truly, Achilles, thou excellest all other men in might and deeds of blood, for the gods themselves protect thee. It may be that Zeus hath given thee to slay all the sons of Troy; nevertheless, depart from me and work thy will upon the plain; for my stream is choked with the multitude of corpses, nor can I pass to the sea. Do thou, therefore, cease from troubling me."

To him Achilles made answer: " This shall be as thou wilt, O Scamander. But the Trojans I will not cease from slaying till I have driven them into their city and have made trial of Hector, whether I shall vanquish him or he shall vanquish me."

And as he spake he sped on, pursuing the Trojans. Then the River cried to Apollo: " Little thou doest the will of thy father, thou of the Silver Bow, who bade thee stand by the men of Troy and help them till darkness should cover the land." And he rushed on with a great wave, stirring together all his streams. The dead bodies he threw upon the shore, roaring as a bull roareth; and them that lived he hid in the depth of his eddies. And all about Achilles rose up the flood, beating full, upon his shield, so that he could not stand fast upon his feet. Then Achilles laid hold of a lime tree, fair and tall, that grew upon the bank; but the tree brake therefrom with all its roots, and tare down the ·bank, and lay across the River, staying its flow, for it had many branches. Thereupon Achilles leapt out of the water and sped across the plain, being sore afraid. But the River ceased not from pursuing him, that he might stay him from slaughter and save the sons of Troy. So far as a man may throw a spear, so far did Achilles leap; strong as an eagle was he, the hunter-bird that is the strongest and swiftest of all birds. And still as he fled the River pursued after him with a great roar. Even as it is with a man that would water his garden, bringing a stream from a fountain; he has a pickaxe in his hand, to break down all that would stay the water; and the stream runs on, rolling the pebbles along with it, and overtakes him that guides it. Even so did the River overtake Achilles, for all that he was swift of foot, for indeed the gods are mightier than men. And when Achilles would have stood against the River, seeking to know whether indeed all the gods were against him, then the great wave smote upon his shoulders; and when he leapt into the air, it bowed his knees beneath him and devoured the ground from under his feet. Then Achilles looked up to heaven and groaned, crying out: "O Zeus, will none of the gods pity me, and save me from the River? I care not what else may befall me. Truly my mother hath deceived me, saying that I should perish under the walls of Troy by the arrows of Apollo. Surely it had been better that Hector should slay me, for he is the bravest of the men of

Troy, but now I shall perish miserably in the River, as some herdboy perisheth whom a torrent sweeps away in a storm."

So he spake; but Poseidon and Athené stood by him, having taken upon them the shape of men, and took him by the hand and strengthened him with comforting words, for Poseidon spake, saying: "Son of Peleus, tremble not, neither be afraid. It is not thy fate to be mastered by the River. He shall soon cease from troubling thee. And do thou heed what we say. Stay not thy hands from the battle, till thou shalt have driven all the sons of Troy that escape thee within the walls of the city. And when thou shalt have slain Hector, go back to the ships; for this day is the day of thy glory."

Then the two departed from him. Now all the plain was covered with water, wherein floated much fair armour and many dead bodies. But Achilles went on even against the stream, nor could the River hold him back; for Athené put great might into his heart. Yet did not Scamander cease from his wrath, but lifted his waves yet higher, and cried aloud to Simois: "Dear brother, let us two stay the fury of this man, or else of a surety he will destroy the city of Priam. Come now, fill all thy streams and rouse thy torrents against him, and lift up against him a mighty wave with a great concourse of tree-trunks and stones, that we may stay this wild man from his fighting. Very high thoughts hath he, even as a god; yet shall neither his might, nor his beauty, nor his fair form profit him; for they shall be covered with much mud; and over himself will I heap abundance of sand beyond all counting. Neither shall the Greeks be able to gather his bones together, with such a heap will I hide them. Surely a great tomb will I build for him; nor will his people have need to make a mound over him when they would bury him."

Then he rushed again upon Achilles, swelling high with foam and blood and dead bodies of men. Very dark was the wave as it rose, and was like to have overwhelmed the man, so that Hera greatly feared for him, lest the River should sweep him away. And she cried to Hephæstus, her son, saying: "Rouse thee,

Haltfoot, my son! I thought that thou wouldst have been a match for Scamander in battle. But come, help us, and bring much fire with thee; and I will call the west wind and the south wind from the sea, with such a storm as shall consume the sons of Troy, both them and their arms. And do thou burn the trees that are by the banks of Xanthus, yea, and the River himself. And let him not turn thee from thy purpose by fury or by craft; but burn till I shall bid thee cease."

Then Hephæstus lit a great fire. First it burned the dead bodies that lay upon the plain, and it dried all the plain, as the north wind in the autumn time dries a field, to the joy of him that tills it. After this it laid hold of the River. The lime tree and the willows and the tamarisks it burned; also the plants that grew in the streams. And the eels and the fishes were sore distressed, twisting hither and thither in the water, being troubled by the breath of Hephæstus. So the might of the River was subdued, and he cried aloud: "O Hephæstus, no one of the gods can match himself with thee. Cease now from consuming me; and Achilles may drive the men of Troy from their city if he will. What have I to do with the strife and sorrow of men?"

So he spake, for all his streams were boiling — as a caldron boils with a great fire beneath it, when a man would melt the fat of a great hog; nor could he flow any longer to the sea, so sorely did the breath of the Fire-god trouble him. Then he cried aloud to Hera, entreating her: "O Hera, why doth thy son torment me only among all? Why should I be blamed more than others that help the men of Troy? Verily, I will cease from helping them, if he also will cease. Nay, I will swear a great oath that I will keep no more the day of doom from the sons of Troy; no, not when all the city shall be consumed with fire."

And Queen Hera heard him, and called to Hephæstus, saying: "Cease, my son; it doth not beseem thee to work such damage to a god for the sake of a mortal man."

So Hephæstus quenched his fire, and the River flowed as he flowed before.

But among the other gods there arose a dreadful strife, for they were divided, the one part against the other. With a great crash they came together, and the broad earth resounded, and the heavens rang as with the voice of a trumpet; and Zeus heard it as he sat on Olympus, and was glad in heart to see the gods join in battle.

First of all, Ares, the shield-piercer, rushed against Athené, holding his spear in his hand, and cried: " Why dost thou make the gods to strive in battle, thou that art bold as a fly and shameless as a dog? Dost thou not remember how thou didst set Diomed, the son of Tydeus, upon me to wound me, and how thou didst take his spear in thy hand, so that all might see it, and drive it through my thigh? Now will I requite thee for all that thou hast done."

And he smote on the ægis shield — the mighty shield that not even the thunder of Zeus can break. But Athené took up in her hand a great stone that lay upon the plain. Black it was and rough, and very great, that men of old had set for a boundary of the field. With this she smote Ares on the neck, that his knees failed beneath him. He lay along the ground, a hundred feet and more, and Athené laughed when she saw him, and cried: "Fool! hast thou not yet learned how much stronger I am than thou, that thou matchest thy might against me? Lie there and suffer the curses of thy mother; for she is wroth because thou hast betrayed the Greeks and helpest the men of Troy."

But Aphrodité took him by the hand, and would have led him away; deep did he groan, and scarce could he gather his spirit together. But when Hera saw it, she cried to Athené, saying: "See now, how Aphrodité would lead Ares out of the battle! Pursue her now, and hinder her."

So Athené pursued after her, and smote her on the breast with her heavy hand; and her knees failed beneath her. So these two lay upon the earth, and Athené cried over them: "Now would that all who help the sons of Troy were as brave and strong as these two. Long since had we ceased from war and destroyed the fair city of Troy."

Then the Great Earthshaker spake to Apollo: "Why stand we apart? Surely this doth not become us, now that the others have joined battle! It were shameful that we should go back to Olympus and have not first fought together. And surely thou art foolish. Dost thou not remember what we suffered, thou and I alone of all the gods, when by the will of Zeus, we served King Laomedon for the space of a year, labouring for wages? I, indeed, built a wall about Troy, broad and very fair, that no man should spoil the city, and thou didst tend the herd of oxen in the glens of Mount Ida. But when the Hours brought the term of our hiring to an end, then did this evil Laomedon rob us of all our hire, and threaten us, and send us away. As for thee, he sware that he would bind thy hands and feet, and sell thee to some far island across the sea. Also, he affirmed that he would cut off the ears of both of us. So we departed, wrathful in heart, and lacking the hire which he promised and paid not. Yet for all this, thou helpest this people, and joinest not thyself to us, that these men of Troy may perish altogether — they and their wives and their children."

To him Apollo made answer: " Earth-

shaker, thou wouldst not call me wise were I
to fight with thee for the sake of miserable
men. For they are but as the leaves. For
to-day they be in the midst of their life, eating
the fruit of the ground, and to-morrow they
perish utterly. Let others strive; but we will
not fight together."

And he turned to depart; for he feared to
join battle with the brother of his sire. But
his sister Artemis, the great huntress of beasts,
was very wroth when she saw him depart,
and rebuked him, crying: "Dost thou fly,
Far-Shooter, and yield the victory to Poseidon? For what then hast thou thy bow?
Never let me hear thee boast again, as thou
hast been wont to boast in the hall of thy
father, that thou wouldst do battle with Poseidon!"

No answer made Apollo; but the wife of
Zeus spake to her in wrath: "How thinkest
thou, shameless one, to stand against me? No
easy one am I for thee to match, for all that
thou hast a bow, and that Zeus hath made
thee a devouring lioness for women to slay
whom thou wilt. 'Tis better for thee to hunt

deer upon the hills than to fight with them that are stronger than thou."

Then did Hera lay her left hand upon the hands of Artemis by the wrist, and with her right hand she took from her her arrows and her bows, and smote her with them about the ears, as she turned away, smiling the while; and the arrows fell from the quiver. And the goddess fled, leaving her bow behind, even as a dove flieth from before a hawk to her hole among the rocks.

Then spake Hermes to Latona: " I will not fight with thee, O Latona! 'Tis a hard thing to strive with them that Zeus hath loved. Boast as thou wilt among the immortal gods that thou hast conquered me in battle."

So he spake; but Latona gathered together the bow and the arrows that had fallen this way and that way in the dust. And Artemis came to Olympus, to the hall of Zeus that is paved with bronze; and, weeping sore, she sat on her father's knee; and her veil was shaken about her with her sobbing. Then her father took her to him, and laughed, and said: " Who, of the dwellers in heaven hath so dealt with thee, my child?"

And Artemis said, "It was Hera, my father, that smote me — Hera, that always maketh strife and quarrel among the immortal gods."

# CHAPTER XXIV.

## THE SLAYING OF HECTOR.

WHILE these things were doing, Achilles ceased not to pursue and slay the men of Troy, and Priam stood on a tower of the wall and saw the people. Sore troubled was he, and he hastened down to the gates and said to the keepers, " Keep the wicket-gates in your hands open, that the people may enter in, for they fly before Achilles." So the keepers held the wicket-gates in their hands, and the people hastened in, wearied with toil and thirst, and covered with dust, and Achilles followed close upon them. And that hour would the Greeks have taken the city of Troy, but that Apollo saved it. For he put courage into the heart of Antenor's son Agenor, standing also by him, that he should not be slain. Therefore Agenor stood, thinking within himself : —

" Shall I now flee with these others? Nay, for not the less will Achilles take me and slay me, and I shall die as a coward dies. Or shall I flee across the plain to Ida, and hide me in the thickets, and come back at nightfall to the city? Yet should he see me he will overtake me and smite me, so swift of foot is he and strong. But what if I stand to meet him before the gates? Well, he, too, is a mortal man, and his flesh may be pierced by the spear."

Therefore he stood till Achilles should come near. And when he came he cast his spear, striking the leg below the knee, but the greave turned off the spear, so strong was it. But when Achilles would have slain him, lo! Apollo lifted him up and set him within the city. And that the men of Troy might have time to enter, he took upon him Agenor's shape. And the false Agenor fled, and Achilles pursued. But meanwhile the men of Troy flocked into the city, nor did they stay to ask who was safe and who was dead, in such haste and fear did they flee. Only Hector remained outside the walls, standing in front of the great Scæan gates. But all the while Achilles was fiercely pursuing the false Agenor, till at last Apollo turned and spake to him : —

"Why dost thou pursue me, swift-footed Achilles? Hast thou not yet found out that I am a god, and that all thy fury is in vain? And now all the sons of Troy are safe in their city, and thou art here, far out of the way, seeking to slay me, who cannot die."

In great wrath Achilles answered him: "Thou hast done me wrong in so drawing me away from the wall, great archer, most mischief-loving of all the gods that are. Had it not been for this, many a Trojan more had bitten the ground. Thou hast robbed me of great glory, and saved thy favourites. O that I had the power to take vengeance on thee! Thou hadst paid dearly for thy cheat!"

Then he turned and rushed towards the city, swift as a race-horse whirls a chariot across the plain. Old Priam spied him from the walls, with his glittering armour, bright as that brightest of the stars — men call it Orion's dog — which shines at vintage-time, a baleful light, bringing the fevers of autumn to men. And the old man groaned aloud when he saw him, and stretching out his hands, cried to his son Hector, where he stood before the gates, eager to do battle with this dread warrior: —

"Wait not for this man, dear son, wait not for him, lest thou die beneath his hand, for indeed he is stronger than thou. Wretch that he is! I would that the gods bare such love to him as I bare! Right soon would the dogs and vultures eat him. Of many brave sons has he bereaved me. Two I miss to-day — Polydorus and Lycaon. May be they are yet alive in the host of the Greeks, and I shall buy them back with gold, of which I have yet great store in my house. And if they are dead, sore grief will it be to me and to the mother who bare them; but little will care the other sons of Troy, so that thou fall not beneath the hand of Achilles. Come within the walls, dear child; come to save the sons and daughters of Troy; come in pity for me, thy father, for whom, in my old age, an evil fate is in store, to see sons slain with the sword, and daughters carried into captivity, and babes dashed upon the ground. Ay, and last of all, the dogs which I have reared in my palace will devour me, lapping my blood and tearing my flesh as

I lie on the threshold of my home. That a young man should fall in battle and suffer such lot as happens to the slain, this is to be borne; but that such dishonour should be done to the white hair and white beard of the old, mortal eyes can see no fouler sight than this."

Thus old Priam spake, but could not turn the heart of his son. And from the wall on the other side of the gate his mother called to him, weeping sore, and if, perchance, she might thus move his pity, she bared her bosom in his sight, and said : —

" Pity me, my son; think of the breast which I gave thee in the old days, and stilled thy cries. Come within the walls; wait not for this man, nor stand in battle against him. If he slay thee, nor I, nor thy wife, shall pay thee the last honours of the dead, but far away by the ships of the Greeks the dogs and vultures will devour thee."

So father and mother besought their son, but all in vain. He was still minded to abide the coming of Achilles. Just as in the mountains a great snake at its hole abides the coming of a man: fierce glare its eyes, and it coils its tail about its hole: so Hector waited for Achilles; and as he waited he thought thus within himself: —

"Woe is me if I go within the walls! Polydamas will be the first to reproach me, for he advised me to bring back the sons of Troy to the city before the night when Achilles roused himself to war. But I would not listen to him. Would that I had! it had been much better for us; but now I have destroyed the people by my folly. I fear the sons and daughters of Troy, what they may say; I fear lest some coward reproach me: 'Hector trusted in his strength, and lo! he has destroyed the people.' Better were it for me either to slay Achilles or to fall by his hand with honour here before the walls. Or stay: shall I put down my shield, and lay aside my helmet, and lean my spear against the wall and go to meet the great Achilles, and promise that we will give back the fair Helen, and all the wealth that Paris carried off with her; ay, and render up all the wealth that there is in the city, that the Greeks may divide it among themselves, binding the sons of Troy with an oath that they keep nothing back? But this is idle talk: he will have no shame or pity, but will slay me while I stand without arms or armour before him. It is not for us to talk as a youth and a maiden talk together. It is better to meet in arms, and see whether the ruler of Olympus will give victory to him or to me."

Thus he thought in his heart; and Achilles came near, brandishing over his right shoulder the great Pelian spear, and the flash of his arms was as the flame of fire, or as the rising sun. And Hector trembled when he saw him, nor dared to abide his coming. Fast he fled from the gates, and fast Achilles pursued him, as a hawk, fastest of all the birds of air, pursues a dove upon the mountains. Past the watch-tower they ran, past the wind-blown fig tree, along the wagon-road which went about the walls, and they came to the fair-flowing fountain where from two springs rises the stream of eddying Scamander. Hot is one spring, and a steam ever goes up from it, as from a burning fire; and cold is the other, cold, even in the summer heats, as hail or snow or ice. There are fair basins of stone, where the wives and fair daughters of Troy were wont to wash their garments, but that was in the old days of peace, or ever the Greeks came to the land. Past the springs they ran, one flying, the other pursuing; brave was he that fled, braver he that pursued; it was no sheep for sacrifice or shield of ox-hide for which they ran, but for the life of Hector, the tamer of horses. Thrice they ran round the city, and all the gods looked on.

And Zeus said: " This is a piteous sight that I behold. My heart is grieved for Hector — Hector, who has ever worshipped me with sacrifice, now on the heights of Ida, and now in the citadel of Troy; and now the great Achilles is pursuing him round the city of Priam. Come, ye gods, let us take counsel together. Shall we save him from death, or let him fall beneath the hand of Achilles?"

Then Athené said: " What is this that thou sayest, great sire? — to rescue a man whom fate has appointed to die? Do it, if it be thy will; but we, the other gods, approve it not."

Zeus answered her: " My heart is loath; yet I would do thee pleasure. Be it as thou wilt."

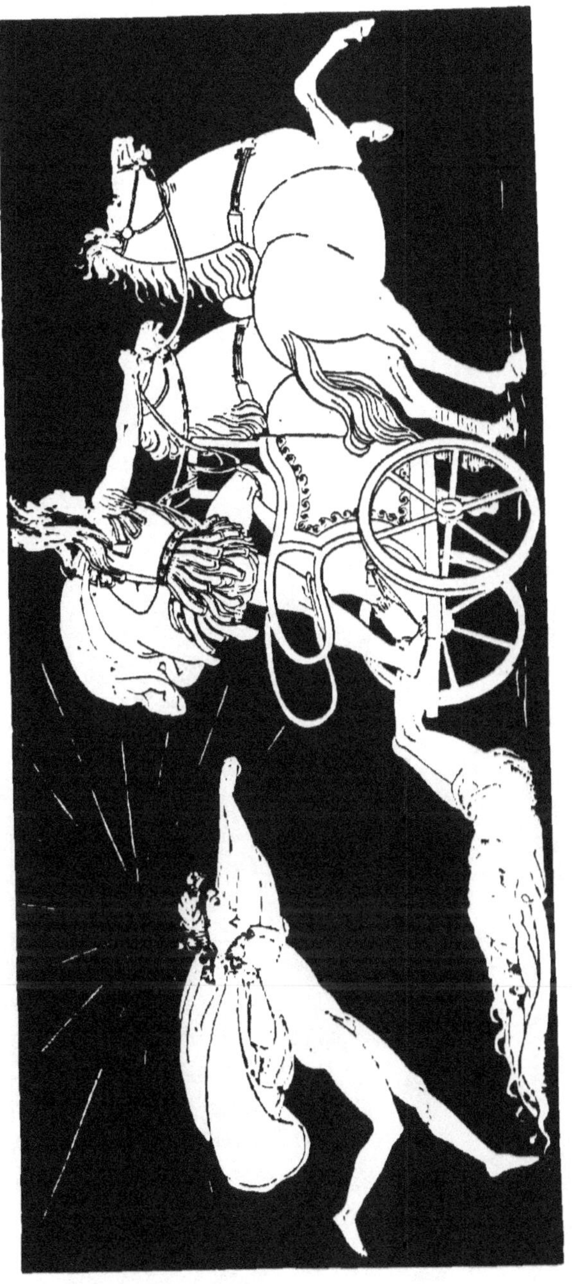

HECTOR'S BODY DRAGGED AT THE CHARIOT OF ACHILLES.

Then Athené came down in haste from the top of Olympus, and still Hector fled and Achilles pursued, just as a dog pursues a fawn upon the hills. And ever Hector made for the gates, or to get shelter beneath the towers, if haply those that stood upon them might defend him with their spears; and ever Achilles would get before him, and drive him towards the plain. So they ran, one making for the city, and the other driving him to the plain. Just as in a dream, when one seems to fly and another seems to pursue, and the one cannot escape and the other cannot overtake, so these two ran together. But as for Hector, Apollo even yet helped him, and gave him strength and nimble knees, else could he not have held out against Achilles, who was swiftest of foot among the sons of men.

Now Achilles had beckoned to the Greeks that no man should throw his spear at Hector, lest, perchance, he should be robbed of his glory. And when the two came in their running for the fourth time to the springs of Scamander, Zeus held out the great balance of doom, and in one scale he put the fate of

Achilles, and in the other the fate of Hector; and lo! the scale of Hector sank down to the realms of death, and Apollo left him.

Then Athené lighted down from the air close to Achilles and said: "This, great Achilles, is our day of glory, for we shall slay Hector, mighty warrior though he be. For it is his doom to die, and not Apollo's self shall save him. But stand thou still and take breath, and I will give this man heart to meet thee in battle."

So Achilles stood leaning upon his spear. And Athené took the shape of Deïphobus, and came near to Hector and said:—

"Achilles presses thee hard, my brother, pursuing thee thus round the city of Priam. Come, let us make a stand and encounter him."

Then Hector answered him, "Deïphobus, I always loved thee best of all my brothers; but now I love thee yet more, for that thou alone, while all others remained within, hast ventured forth to stand by my side."

But the false Deïphobus said: "Much did father and mother and all my comrades beseech me to remain. But my heart was sore troubled for thee, and I could not stay. But let us stand and fight this man, not stinting our spears, and see whether he shall carry our spoil to the ships, or we shall slay him here."

Then the two chiefs came near to each other, and Hector with the waving plume spake first, and said: " Thrice, great Achilles, hast thou pursued me round the walls of Troy, and I dared not stand up against thee; but now I fear thee no more. Only let us make this covenant between us: if Zeus give me the victory, I will do no dishonour to thy body; thy arms and armour will I take, and give back thy body to the Greeks; and do thou promise to do likewise."

But Achilles scowled at him and said: " Hector, talk not of covenants to me. Men and lions make no oaths between each other, neither is there any agreement between wolves and sheep. So there shall be no covenant between me and thee. One of us two shall fall; and now is the time for thee to show thyself a warrior, for of a truth Athené will slay thee by my spear, and thou shalt pay the penalty for all my comrades whom thou hast slain."

Then he threw the mighty spear, but Hector saw it coming and avoided it, crouching on the ground, so that the mighty spear flew above his head and fixed itself in the earth. But Athené snatched it from the ground and gave it back to Achilles, Hector not perceiving.

Then Hector spake to Achilles: "Thou hast missed thy aim, great Achilles. It was no word of Zeus that thou spakest, prophesying my doom, but thou soughtest to cheat me, terrifying me by thy words. Thou shalt not drive thy steel into my back, but here into my breast, if the gods will it so. But now look out for my spear. Would it might bury itself in thy flesh! The battle would be easier for the men of Troy were thou only out of the way."

And as he spake he threw his long-shafted spear. True aim he took, for the spear struck the very middle of Achilles' shield. It struck, but pierced it not, but bounded far away, for the shield was not of mortal make. And

ANDROMACHÉ FAINTING ON THE WALL.

Hector stood dismayed, for he had not another spear, and when he called to Deïphobus that he should give him another, lo! Deïphobus was gone. Then Hector knew that his end was come, and he said to himself : " Now have the gods called me to my doom. I thought that Deïphobus was near; but he is within the walls, and the help which he promised me was but a cheat with which Athené cheated me. Zeus and Apollo are with me no more; but if I must die, let me at least die in such a deed as men of after time may hear of."

So he spake, and drew the mighty sword that hung by his side: then as an eagle rushes through the clouds to pounce on a leveret or a lamb, he rushed on the great Achilles. But he dealt never a blow; for Achilles charged to meet him, his shield before his breast, his helmet bent forward as he ran, with the long plumes streaming behind, and the gleam of his spear-point was as the gleam of the evening star, which is the fairest of all the stars in heaven. One moment he thought where he should drive it home, for the armour which Hector had won from Patroclus guarded him well; but one spot there was, where by the collar-bone the neck joins the shoulder (and nowhere is the stroke of sword or spear more deadly). There he drave in the spear, and the point stood out behind the neck, and Hector fell in the dust.

Then Achilles cried aloud: " Hector, thou thoughtest in the day when thou didst spoil Patroclus of his arms that thou wouldst be safe from vengeance, taking, forsooth, no account of me. And lo! thou art fallen before me, and now the dogs and vultures shall devour thee, but to him all the Greeks shall give due burial."

But Hector, growing faint, spake to him: " Nay, great Achilles, by thy life, and by thy knees, and by thy parents dear, I pray thee, let not the dogs of the Greeks devour me. Take rather the ransom, gold and bronze, that my father and mother shall pay thee, and let the sons and daughters of Troy give me burial rites."

But Achilles scowled at him, and cried: " Dog, seek not to entreat me! I could mince that flesh of thine and devour it raw, such grief hast thou wrought me. Surely the dogs shall devour thee, nor shall any man hinder. No ransom, though it were ten times told, should buy thee back; no, not though Priam should offer thy weight in gold."

Then Hector, who was now at the point to die, spake to him: "I know thee well, what manner of man thou art, that the heart in thy breast is iron only. Only beware lest some vengeance from the gods come upon thee in the day when Paris and Apollo shall slay thee, for all thy valour, by the Scæan gates."

So speaking, he died. But Achilles said, "Die, hound; but my fate I meet when Zeus and the other gods decree."

Then he drew his spear out of the corpse, and stripped off the arms; and all the Greeks came about the dead man, marvelling at his stature and beauty, and no man came but wounded the dead corpse. And one would say to another, "Surely this Hector is less dreadful now than in the day when he would burn our ships with fire."

Then Achilles devised a ruthless thing in his heart. He pierced the ankle-bones of Hector, and so bound the body with thongs of ox-hide to the chariot, letting the head drag behind, the head that once was so fair, and now was so disfigured in the dust. So he dragged Hector to the ships. And Priam saw him from the walls, and scarce could his sons keep him back, but that he should go forth and beg the body of his dear son from him who had slain him. And Hecuba, his mother, also bewailed him, but Andromaché knew not as yet of what had befallen. For she sat in her dwelling, wearing a great purple mantle broidered with flowers. And she bade her maidens make ready a bath for Hector, when he should come back from the battle, nor knew that he should never need it more. But the voice of wailing from the town came to her, and she rose up hastily in great fear, and dropped the shuttle from her hand, and called to her maidens:—

"Come with me, ye maidens, that I may see what has befallen, for I heard the voice of Queen Hecuba, and I fear me much that some evil has come to the children of Priam. For it may be that Achilles has run between Hector and the city, and is pursuing him to the plain, for never will Hector abide with the army, but will fight in the front, so bold is he."

Then she hasted through the city like as she were mad. And when she came to the wall, she stood and looked; and lo! the horses of Achilles were dragging Hector to the ships. Then did darkness come on her, and she fell back fainting, and from her fair head dropped the net and the wreath and the diadem which golden Aphrodité gave her on the day when Hector of the waving plume took her from the house of Eëtion to be his wife.

# CHAPTER XXV.

### THE BURNING OF PATROCLUS.

WHILE the Trojans mourned for Hector in the city, the Greeks went back to the camp. All the others were scattered, each to his own ship, but Achilles spake to the Myrmidons, saying, " Loose not your horses from the yoke, but let us do honour to Patroclus, driving our chariots round the dead, and making lamentation the while."

Then the Myrmidons did as he had bidden them ; thrice round the dead they drave their chariots, and made lamentation ; and Achilles led the mourning. Also he laid the body of Hector in the dust beside the dead. After that he made a funeral feast for his people. He himself was brought by the chiefs, much against his will, to King Agamemnon, who had made a great feast for the leaders of the Greeks. But when the heralds heated water in a caldron, and would have had him wash off the blood, he refused, saying: "Nay; water shall not come nigh me till I have laid Patroclus on the fire, and heaped a mound over him. Now let us eat our meal, though it be in sorrow; to-morrow we will pay due honour to the dead."

So they ate and drank; and when they had had enough, the others lay down to sleep, each in his own tent, but Achilles lay groaning heavily amidst the Myrmidons in an open place by the sea.

While he slept, the shade of Patroclus stood above his head. The very same was he in stature, and voice, and height, yea, even in the garments that he wore. The spirit spake, saying: "Sleepest thou, Achilles, and forgettest me? Bury me speedily, for the spirits of the dead suffer me not to be with them, but I wander alone in Hades. And give me now thine hand, for never shall we two sit apart and hold counsel together, for I shall come again no more from the dead after that the fire hath consumed me. Lay also thy bones with mine, that we may be together, even as when we grew together, thou a lad and I a lad, in thy father's hall."

Then Achilles stretched out his hands, but caught not the ghost, for it fled as a smoke flieth.

The next day they made a great pile of wood, and laid the dead man thereon. Nine dogs had the Prince, and Achilles slew two of them on the pile, and four horses he slew, and also the twelve youths of Troy whom he had taken at the river. Then he set fire to the pile, saying: " Hear, Patroclus; twelve of the sons of Troy doth the fire devour with thee; but Hector will I give to the dogs."

And when the burning was well-nigh ended, Achilles spake, saying: " Quench ye the fire that yet remains with wine, and gather the bones of Patroclus together where they lie apart in the midst of the pile, and put them in an urn of gold against the day of my death. And make over them a tomb not over large; but when I am dead also, then shall ye that are left make it higher, as is meet."

And when all these things were ended, Achilles, willing to do all honour to the dead man, would have games, wherein the chiefs should contend one with the other. So, having called the people together, he brought forth out his ships many things that should be for prizes, — caldrons, kettles of bronze, and horses and mules, and fair women-slaves, and iron.

First, he would have a contest of chariots and horses, for which he set forth three prizes: For the first, a woman-slave, skilled in all the works of the loom, and with her a kettle of bronze with three feet, of twenty and two measures; and for the second, a mare of six years old; and for the third, a kettle of bronze, of four measures, fair and new; and for the fourth, two talents of gold; and for the fifth, a double cup; then he stood up in the midst, and spake: "Ye men of Greece, behold these prizes, which I have set in the midst for a race of chariots. Now know ye that if we were doing honour to another than Patroclus, I myself should carry the first prize to my tent, for there are not in the camp horses such as mine; and, indeed, they are not of mortal breed, but Poseidon gave them to Peleus, my father. But from this race I stand apart, and they also; for he that drave them is dead, whom they loved; therefore they stand grieving sore, and their manes droop to the ground. But contend together ye that will." Then stood up five chiefs; first of all, Eumelus, who was the son of Admetus, and Alcestis his wife, and next to him Diomed, having horses of Troy, which he took from Æneas (but Æneas himself Apollo delivered from death); and third, Menelaüs, driving his horse Whitefoot, and a mare, Flash-of-Fire, which Echepolus of Sicyon gave to King Agamemnon, that he might not sail to Troy, but might tarry at home, for he was very rich. Fourth came Antilochus, son of Nestor of Pylos, and after him Meriones.

Then said Nestor, the old man, to Antilochus: "My son, the gods have given thee skill in driving, wherefore there is small need to teach thee. But thy horses are not swift as those with whom thou contendest, and I fear much that thou wilt suffer defeat. Yet may counsel avail much, by which others also, as woodmen and pilots, excel. For one man, trusting in his chariot and his horses, that they are good, suffereth them to stray over the plain; but another looketh ever unto the turning-post, that he go not far from it, and holdeth well the reins and watcheth him that is before. And now heed what I say. There is a stump of a tree, a fathom high, and by it two white stones, the tomb of some man of old, or may be a boundary. There hath Achilles set the point of turning. To this keep thou as close as may be, leaning thyself to the left in thy chariot. And thy off horse thou must smite with the goad and shout to him, loosing the rein, but the near thou must press close to the stump, till the nave of the wheel be close to it; but touch not the stones, lest thou frighten thy horses and break thy chariot. And be sure that if thou art first here, no man shall pass thee afterwards, not though he drave Arion, which was the horse of Adrastus, or the horses of King Laomedon."

After this they drew lots for their places. And the first lot fell to Antilochus, and after him came Eumelus, and Menelaüs, and Meriones, and Diomed, in this order. Then Achilles marked the course, making old Phœnix the judge. After this the race began, and the men lifted their whips and smote their horses, and shouted also. And the dust rose up beneath the horses' breasts, and their manes were blown by the wind, and the chariots were seen now low upon the earth and now high in the air. But when they were come near to the end of the course at the turning-point, it might be seen which steeds were the better. For the horses of Eumelus were foremost, and next to these the horses of King Diomed, very close, so that they seemed about to step upon the chariot that was before them, and the back and broad shoulders of Eumelus were hot with breath, their heads being close upon him. And, indeed, Diomed had now passed him, or been equal in the race, but Apollo grudged him the victory,—for the god loved him not,— and struck the whip out of his hand. Very wroth was Diomed, and his eyes were filled with tears, that his horses should thus lack control. But Athené saw the thing and had pity on him, and gave him back the whip, and put strength into his horses. Also she went near to the son of Admetus, and brake the yoke of his chariot, so that the pole smote upon the ground, and the man himself was

thrown down, having his elbows and mouth
and nostrils sorely bruised, and a wound on
his forehead over the eyebrows. Then did
Diomed take the first place with his chariot,
and next to him came Menelaüs. But Antilochus cried to his horses, saying: " Now
speed ye as best ye can. I bid you not strive
with the horses of King Diomed, for Athené
giveth them swiftness and strength; but the
horses of Menelaüs ye can overtake. It were
a shame to you that Flame-of-Fire, being a
mare, should surpass you. Nay, hear me. If
ye be worsted in this, to Nestor ye shall not
return, for I will slay you here with my sword."
And the horses feared the fury of the
Prince, and leapt forward. Now Antilochus
had spied a narrow place in the way, where it
had been broken by the floods in the winter;
and as Menelaüs drove his chariot thereby,
Antilochus, turning a little out of the way,
sought to pass at the same time. Now there
was not space sufficient for two chariots, and
Menelaüs feared, and cried: " Why drivest
thou so madly, Antilochus? Stay awhile, and
thou canst pass me if thou wilt, where the way

is broader ; but now thou wilt hurt thy chariot and mine." But Antilochus drave the more furiously, making as though he heard not. And for the space of a quoit's throw the chariots were abreast, but then Menelaüs held back, fearing lest they should clash together. But he cried to Antilochus : " Was there ever man so evil-minded as thou ? Yet shalt thou not win this prize unless thou shalt forswear thyself that thou hast dealt fairly." And to his horses cried : " Speed ye ! Stand not still; ye shall overtake them, for they will grow weary before you."

In the meantime the Greeks sat waiting till the chariots should come back. And Idomeneus of Crete espied them first, for he sate apart from the crowd, where the ground was higher. Then he said, — for he noted one horse that was bay, with a great circle of white, like unto the moon, upon his forehead, — " Do ye also see these chariots, men of Greece ? For surely the order is changed, and he is not foremost that was so, but some mishap hath befallen him on the way. But it may be that my eyes see not as well as they were wont.

Look ye, therefore; for I know not who cometh first, yet do I think that it is Diomed, son of Tydeus."

Then spoke Ajax Oïleus, swift of foot: "Why talkest thou thus idly, and before the time? Thou art not the youngest among the Greeks, nor thine eyes the keenest. The horses are yet foremost that were at the first, and the charioteer is Eumelus."

Then Idomeneus, in great wrath, made reply: "Ajax, thou art ready to strive and fierce of speech, for in naught else dost thou excel. Come, let us wager a kettle of bronze or a caldron, and Agamemnon shall judge. So when thou payest thou wilt learn wisdom."

But when Ajax would have answered him again, Achilles suffered him not, but made peace between them. Then came in Diomed first of all, and leapt from the chariot; and next to him Antilochus, having surpassed Menelaüs by craft and not by speed; nor, indeed, was Menelaüs far behind, being as near to him as a chariot is near to the horse which draweth it, so swift was the mare Flame-of-Fire, for at the first he had been a whole

quoit's throw behind.  But Meriones was vanquished by the flight of a spear, for his horses
were the slowest, and he himself less skilled to
drive.  Last of all came Eumelus, drawing his
chariot, and driving his horses before him.
And Achilles pitied him, and said: "The
most skilful cometh last.  Surely he shall have
the second prize."

And the Greeks gave consent; but Antilochus cried aloud: "Wilt thou take away this
prize from me because his chariot was broken?
Had he prayed to the gods, this had not
happened.  But if thou pitiest him, give him
somewhat of thine own.  As for this prize, no
man taketh it from me but by arms."

And Achilles laughed and said: "'Tis well
said, Antilochus.  I will give him of mine own,
even a breastplate which Asteropæus wore."

Then stood up Menelaüs, in great wrath,
and said: "What is this that thou hast done,
Antilochus?  For thou hast shamed me and
my horses, putting thine own in front, which
are, of a truth, much worse than they.  Judge,
therefore, between us, ye chiefs of the Greeks.
And thou, Antilochus, stand before thy chariot

and thy horses, as the custom is, holding in one hand thy whip, and laying the other hand on thine horses, and swear by Poseidon that thou didst not hinder my chariot by fraud."

To him Antilochus made reply: "Bear with me, Menelaüs, for I am younger than thou, and thou knowest how young men go astray, for their judgment is hasty and their wit small. And as for the mare, I give it thee, and aught else that thou desirest, rather than that I should be at strife with thee or sin against the gods."

And the soul of Menelaüs was glad, as the corn is glad when the dew falleth upon it; and he said: "This is well said, son of Nestor. And now — for thy father and thy brother have borne much for my sake — I give thee this mare."

And he himself took the kettle of bronze, and the fourth prize Meriones had; but the double cup Achilles gave to old Nestor, saying: "Take this to be a memorial of the burial of Patroclus, whom thou wilt not see any more. For I know that old age hinders thee, that thou canst not contend in wrestling or boxing with the rest."

And the old man gave him thanks, and told what marvellous things he had done in his youth; that no man had vanquished him in wrestling, or in boxing, or in the race, or in casting the spear; only in the chariot-race he had been surpassed, and that by craft, for the two sons of Actor rode together, and one held the reins and the other plied the whip.

After this Achilles set forth two prizes for boxers: for the conqueror a mule, and for him that should be vanquished a cup with two mouths. Then stood up Epeüs, the son of Panopeus, and spake: "Who desireth to take this cup? for the mule no man but I shall have. In battle I am weak — for what man can do all things? — but whosoever shall stand against me to-day, verily, I will tear his flesh and break his bones, so that his friends had best be at hand to carry him away."

Then there rose up against him Euryalus, son of Mecisteus, a man of Argos. King Diomed stood by him, wishing much that he might prevail, and brought him his girdle that he might gird himself, and gave him the great gloves of bull's hide. Then the two stood together in the midst. Many blows did they deal to each other, so that the noise was dreadful to hear, and the sweat ran down from them. But after a while Epeüs sprang forward and smote Euryalus on the jaw, even through his guard, and Euryalus could not stand against him; but even as a fish is dashed by the north wind against the shore, so was he dashed to the earth. But Epeüs raised him up, and his companions led him away, sorely wounded and amazed.

After this Achilles would have a match of wrestling, saying that the conqueror should have a great kettle of bronze, of twelve oxen's worth, and the vanquished a woman-slave, skilful at the loom, worth four oxen. Then stood up Ajax the Greater and Ulysses, and took hold of one another with their hands, and strove together for the mastery. But after a while, when neither could prevail, and the people were weary with looking, Ajax spake, saying: "Come, Ulysses; thou shalt lift me from the ground if thou canst, and I thee. So shall we finish this matter." Then Ajax laid hold of Ulysses to lift him; and this he had done, but Ulysses used craft, as was his wont, and put forth his leg and smote Ajax on the sinew behind the knee, so that he fell, and Ulysses also above him. Then Ulysses would have lifted Ajax from the ground; a little space he moved him, but lifted him not, and his knee yielded beneath him, and they fell to the ground, both of them. But when they would have striven the third time, Achilles hindered them, saying: "Hold! it is enough. Ye are conquerers both, and your prizes shall be equal."

Next to this was a trial of racers on foot, in which three contended, Ajax the Less, and Ulysses, and Antilochus. Three also were the prizes; first of all, a great mixing-bowl of silver; six measures it held, nor was there aught fairer upon earth. In Sidon was it wrought, and Phœnician merchants brought it over the sea and gave it King Thoas; and Euneus, who was son of Hypsipyle, daughter to Thoas, gave it to Patroclus to be a ransom of Lycaon, son of King Priam. And for the second winner was a well-fattened ox, and for the third half a talent of gold. From the point where the chariots had turned in the race they ran, and in a short space Ajax the Less was foremost, with Ulysses close upon him, close as is the shuttle to the breast of a woman who stands at the loom and weaves. Hard behind him he ran, treading in his steps before the dust could rise from them. And when they were now drawing to the end of the course Ulysses prayed to Athené that she should help him, and Athené heard him, and made his knees and feet right nimble, and even at the very end she caused that Ajax slipped in the filth where certain oxen had been slain, so that his mouth and nostrils were filled with it. So Ulysses gained the mixing-bowl; but Ajax stood and spat the filth from his mouth, and laid his hand on the head of the ox, and cried, " Surely the goddess caused my feet to slip, for she ever standeth by Ulysses, and helpeth him as a mother helpeth a child."

So he spake, and all men laughed to hear him; and last of all came Antilochus, taking the third prize. And he said: " Ye know well, my friends, that the immortal gods ever help the aged. As for Ajax, he is but a little older than I, but Ulysses is of another generation.

T

Yet is his verily a green old age; hardly may any of the Greeks strive with him, but only Achilles himself."

This was Achilles well pleased to hear, and said: "Thou shalt not praise me in vain, Antilochus. Take now another half talent to thy half."

And he gave him the gold, and Antilochus took it, and was glad.

Then did Achilles set in the midst a long-shafted spear, and a shield, and a helmet. The arms of Sarpedon they were, which Patroclus had taken from him on the plain of Troy, in the day wherein he also had been slain. And he spake, saying: "Now let two chiefs, such as are the bravest among the men of Greece, come forth and fight for the mastery, having armed themselves as if for the battle. And it shall be that he who shall first pierce the skin of him that standeth against him shall have the victory. To him will I give this sword, with studs of silver, fair work of Thrace, which I took from the great Asteropæus. As for these arms, the two shall divide them. Also to both will I give a great banquet in my tent."

Then stood up to contend together Ajax, the son of Telamon, and Diomed, son of Tydeus. Three times did they charge each other; and Ajax drave his spear through Diomed's shield, but the skin he touched not, for the breastplate hindered him. But Diomed smote with his spear over the edge of the shield at the neck of Ajax. Then were the Greeks sore afraid for the hero, and cried out that the battle should cease, and that the two should have equal rewards. Nevertheless, the victory was counted to Diomed, and Achilles gave him the sword with the scabbard, and also the belt thereof.

Then took Achilles a great weight of iron for a quoit, which had been King Eëtion's, who was the father of Andromaché, Hector's wife. And he said: " He who shall cast this the farthest shall have it for his own. And, verily, he that hath it, though his field be very wide, shall not lack for iron. Five years shall it last, so that neither shepherd nor ploughman shall have need to go to the town to buy.

Then there rose up to contend Polypœtes, who was of the race of the Lapithæ, and Leonteus, his comrade, also Ajax, the son of Telamon, and Epeüs. And first Epeüs cast it, and all the Greeks laughed, for he cast it not far, for all that he was so strong; and after him Leonteus made trial of it, and next Ajax, overpassing the marks of them that had gone before. But when Polypœtes stood up, lo! he cast it as far beyond the others as a herdsman flings his staff among his herd. And all the people shouted, and the comrades of Polypœtes rose up and bare the prize to the ships.

And after this the archers contended together, and the prize for the first was ten axes of iron, with an edge on either side; and for the second ten axes also, but having one edge only. Now the two that strove were Teucer, who was the brother of Ajax the Greater, and Meriones, who was the comrade of King Idomeneus of Crete. The mark that was set for them was the mast of a ship which Achilles had set up far off in the sands by the sea, to the top whereof he had bound a wood-dove, having a cord about its foot. And the lot fell to Teucer that he should shoot the first, and he shot, drawing the bow mightily; but he prayed not to Apollo, nor vowed that he would offer to him a sacrifice of a hundred lambs. The bird he hit not, for this Apollo gave not to him; but he smote the cord wherewith the dove was bound, and divided it; and the bird flew into the air, and the Greeks clapped their hands to see it. Then did Meriones take the bow from his hand, — for they shot with the same, the two of them, — and the arrow he had made ready before against his turn. Also he vowed a sacrifice of a hundred lambs to King Apollo. Then he beheld, and lo! the dove was very high in the clouds above his head, and he shot, and the arrow smote it under the wing as it wheeled in the air, and passed right through it. Before the feet of the archer fell the arrow, and the bird lighted on the mast. Then speedily it died, so that it fell upon the ground. So Meriones took the double-edged axes, and Teucer them that had one edge only.

Then there was a contest of throwing the spear; and the prize was a long-shafted spear, and a caldron that had never felt the fire, of the worth of an ox. For this there stood up King Agamemnon and Meriones, who was the comrade of King Idomeneus. But when Achilles saw the two, he spake, saying: " King Agamemnon, all men know that thou excellest in strength. Take thou this prize for thyself; and, if thou wilt, we will give a spear to Meriones."

And the saying pleased King Agamemnon. So the Games of Patroclus were ended; and the people were scattered to the ships, and sat down to eat and drink; and afterwards they slept. But Achilles slept not, for he remembered his dear Patroclus, and all that the two had done and endured together, journeying over sea and land, and standing against the enemy in the day of battle.

# CHAPTER XXVI.

## THE RANSOMING OF HECTOR.

WHEN the burial of Patroclus was ended, the gods held council about Hector, for Achilles did despite to the body of Hector, dragging it about the tomb of his friend, but the gods had pity on the dead man, because in his life he had ever honoured them.

Then did Zeus send for Thetis, and when she was come to Olympus, he said: " Get thee to the camp, and bid thy son give up Hector for ransom, for I am wroth with him because he doth despite to the dead."

So Thetis went to Achilles, and found him weeping softly for his dead friend, for the strength of his sorrow was now spent, and she said to him: " It is the will of the gods that thou give up the body of Hector, and take in exchange the ransom of gold and precious things which his father will give thee for him."

And her son answered, " Be it so, if the gods will have it."

Then Zeus sent Iris, who was his messenger, to King Priam, where he sat with his face wrapped in his mantle, and his sons weeping about him, and his daughters wailing through the chambers of his palace.

Then Iris spake : " Be of good cheer, Priam, son of Dardanus; Zeus has sent me to thee. Go, taking with thee such gifts as may best please the heart of Achilles, and bring back the body of thy dear son Hector. Go without fear of death or harm, and go alone. Only let an aged herald be with thee, to help thee when thou bringest back the body of the dead."

Then Priam rose with joy, and bade his sons bring forth his chariot; but first he went to his chamber, and called to Hecuba, his wife, and told her of his purpose, nor heeded when she sought to turn him from it, but said: " Seek not to hold me back, nor be a bird of evil omen in my house. If any prophet or seer had bidden me do this thing, I should have held it a deceit; but now have I heard the very voice of the messenger of Zeus.

Wherefore, I shall go. And if I die, what care I? Let Achilles slay me, so that I embrace once more the body of my son."

Then he bade put into a wagon shawls and mantles that had never been washed, and rugs, and cloaks, and tunics, twelve of each, and ten talents of gold, and two bright three-footed caldrons, and four basins, and a cup of passing beauty which the Thracians had given him. The old man spared nothing that he had, if only he might buy back his son. None of the Trojans would he suffer to come near him. " Begone," he cried, " ye cowards! Have ye nothing to wail for at home, that ye come to wail with me? Surely, an easy prey will ye be to the Greeks, now that Hector is dead."

Then he cried with like angry words to his sons, Paris, and Agathon, and Deïphobus, and the others — there were nine of them in all : —

" Make haste, ye evil brood. Would that ye all had died in the room of Hector. Surely, an ill-fated father am I. Many a brave son I had, as Mestor, and Troilus, and Hector, who was fairer than any of the sons of men. But all these are gone, and only the cowards are left, masters of lying words, and skilful in the dance, and mighty to drink wine.  But go, yoke the mules to the wagon."

So they yoked the mules to the wagon. But the horses for his chariot Priam, with the herald, yoked himself.

Then Hecuba came near, and bade a woman-servant come and pour water on his hands.  And when she had poured, King Priam took a great cup from the hands of his wife, and made a libation to Zeus, and prayed : —

" Hear me, Father Zeus, and grant that Achilles may pity me.  And do thou send me now a lucky sign, that I may go with a good heart to the ships of the Greeks."

And Zeus heard him, and sent an eagle, a mighty bird, whose wings spread out on either side as wide as is the door of some spacious chamber in a rich man's house.  On his right hand it flew high above the city; and all rejoiced when they saw the sign.

Then the old man mounted his chariot in haste, and drove forth from the palace.  Before him the mules drew the four-wheeled wagon, and these the herald Idæus guided. But his chariot the old King drove himself. And all his kinsfolk went with him, weeping as for one who was going to his death. But when they came down from the city to the plain, Priam and the herald went towards the ships of the Greeks, but all the others returned to Troy.

But Zeus saw him depart, and said to Hermes: " Hermes, go guide King Priam to the ships of the Greeks, so that no man see him before he comes to the tents of Achilles."

Then Hermes fastened on his feet the fair sandals of gold with which he flies, fast as the wind, over sea and land, and in his hand he took the rod with which he opens and closes, as he wills, the eyes of men. And he flew down and lighted on the plain of Troy, taking on him the likeness of a fair youth.

But when they had driven past the great Tomb of Ilus, they stopped the horses and the mules, to let them drink of the river. And darkness came over the land; and then the herald spied Hermes, and said : —

" Consider, my lord, what we shall do. I see a man, and I am sore afraid lest he slay us. Shall we flee on the chariot, or shall we go near and entreat him, that he may have pity upon us?"

Then the old man was sore troubled, and his hair stood up with fear. But Hermes came near and took him by the hand and said : —

"Whither goest thou, old man, with thy horses and mules through the darkness? Hast thou no fear of these fierce Greeks, who are close at hand? If any one should see thee with all this wealth, what then? And thou art not young, nor is thy attendant young, that ye should defend yourselves against an enemy. But I will not harm thee, nor suffer any other, for thou art like my own dear father."

"It is well, my son," said the old man. "Surely one of the blessed gods is with me, in causing me to meet such an one as thou, so fair and so wise. Happy the parents of such a son!"

And Hermes said: "Come, tell me true, old man. Are you sending away all these treasures that they may be kept safe for you far away? or are all the men of Troy leaving the city, seeing -now that Hector, who was their bravest warrior, is dead ?"

Then Priam answered, "Who art thou, my son, and what thy race, that thou speakest so truly about my hapless son ?"

"Often," said Hermes, "have I seen Hector in the battle, both at other times, and when he drove the Greeks before him at the ships. We, indeed, stood and watched and marvelled at him, for Achilles would not suffer us to fight, being wroth with King Agamemnon. Now I am a follower of Achilles, coming from Greece in the same ship with him. One of the Myrmidons I am, son of Polyctor, an old man such as thou art. Six other sons he has, and when we drew lots who should come to the war, it fell to me. But know that with the morning the Greeks will set their battle in array against the city, for they are weary of their sojourn, and the kings cannot keep them back."

Then said Priam, " If thou art an attendant of Achilles, tell me true, is my son yet by the ships, or have the dogs devoured him ?"

And Hermes answered: " Nor dogs nor vultures have devoured him. Still he lies by the ships of Achilles; and though this is the twelfth day since he was slain, no decay has touched him. Nay, though Achilles drags him round the tomb of his dear Patroclus, yet even so does no unseemliness come to him. All fresh he lies, and the blood is washed from him, and all his wounds are closed — and many spear-points pierced him. The blessed gods love him well, dead man though he be."

This King Priam was well pleased to hear. "It is well," he said, "for a man to honour the gods; for, indeed, as my son never forgot the dwellers on Olympus, so have they not forgotten him, even in death. But do thou take this fair cup, and do kindness to him, and lead me to the tent of Achilles."

"Nay," answered Hermes; "thou speakest this in vain. No gift would I take from thy hand unknown to Achilles; for I honour him much, and fear to rob him, lest some evil happen to me afterwards. But thee I will guide to Argos itself, if thou wilt, whether by land or sea, and no one shall blame my guiding."

Then he leapt into the chariot of the King

and caught the reins in his hand, and gave the horses and the mules a strength that was not their own. And when they came to the ditch and the trench that guarded the ships, lo! the guards were busy with their meal; but Hermes made sleep descend upon them, and opened the gates, and brought in Priam with his treasures. And when they came to the tent of Achilles, Hermes lighted down from the chariot and said:—

"Lo! I am Hermes, whom my Father Zeus hath sent to be thy guide. And now I shall depart, for I would not that Achilles should see me. But go thou in, and clasp his knees, and beseech him by his father, and his mother, and his child. So shalt thou move his heart with pity."

So Hermes departed to Olympus, and King Priam leapt down from the chariot, leaving the herald to care for the horses and the mules, and went to the tent. There he found Achilles sitting; his comrades sat apart, but two waited on him, for he had but newly ended his meal, and the table was yet at his hand. But no man saw King Priam till he was close to Achilles, and caught his knees and kissed his hands, the dreadful, murderous hands that had slain so many of his sons. As a man who slays another by mishap flies to some stranger land, to some rich man's home, and all wonder to see him, so Achilles wondered to see King Priam, and his comrades wondered, looking one at another. Then King Priam spake:—

"Think of thy father, godlike Achilles, and pity me. He is old, as I am, and, it may be, his neighbours trouble him, seeing that he has no defender; yet so long as he knows that thou art alive, it is well with him, for every day he hopes to see his dear son returned from Troy. But as for me, I am altogether wretched. Many a valiant son I had,—nineteen born to me of one mother,—and most of them are dead, and he that was the best of all! who kept our city safe, he has been slain by thee. He it is whom I have come to ransom. Have pity on him and on me, thinking of thy father. Never, surely, was lot so sad as this, to kiss the hands that slew a son."

But the words so stirred the heart of Achilles that he wept, thinking now of Patroclus, and now of his old father at home; and Priam wept, thinking of his dead Hector. But at last Achilles stood up from his seat and raised King Priam, having pity on his white hair and his white beard, and spake: —

"How didst thou dare to come to the ships of the Greeks, to the man who slew thy sons? Surely, thou must have a heart of iron. But sit thou down: let our sorrows rest in our hearts, for there is no profit in lamentation. It is the will of the gods that men should suffer woe, but they are themselves free from care. Two chests are set by the side of Father Zeus, one of good and one of evil gifts, and he mixes the lot of men, taking out of both. Many noble gifts did the gods give to King Peleus: wealth and bliss beyond that of other men, and kingship over the Myrmidons. Ay! and they gave him a goddess to be his wife. But they gave also this evil, that he had no stock of stalwart children in his house, but one son only, and I cannot help him at all in his old age, for I tarry here far away in Troy. Thou, too, old man, hadst wealth and power of old, and lordship over all that lies between Lesbos and Phrygia and the stream of Hellespont. And to thee the gods have given this ill, that there is ever battle and slaughter about thy city walls. But as for thy son, wail not for him, for thou canst not raise him up."

But Priam answered: "Make me not to sit, great Achilles, while Hector lies unhonoured. Let me ransom him, and look upon him with my eyes, and do thou take the gifts. And the gods grant thee to return safe to thy father-land."

But Achilles frowned and said: "Vex me not; I am minded myself to give thee back thy Hector. For my mother came from the sea, bearing the bidding of Zeus, and thou, methinks, hast not come hither without some guidance from the gods. But trouble me no more, lest I do thee some hurt."

And King Priam feared and held his peace. Then Achilles hastened from his tent, and two comrades with him. First they loosed the horses from the chariot and the mules from the wagon; then they brought in the herald Idæus, and took the gifts. Only they left of them two cloaks and a tunic, wherein they might wrap the dead. And Achilles bade the women wash and anoint the body, but apart from the tent, lest, perchance, Priam should see his son and cry aloud, and so awaken the fury in his heart. But when it was washed and anointed, Achilles himself lifted it in his arms and put it on the litter, and his comrades lifted the litter on the wagon.

And when all was finished, Achilles groaned and cried to his dead friend, saying: —

"Be not wroth, Patroclus, if thou shouldst hear in the unknown land that I have ransomed Hector to his father: a noble ransom hath he paid me, and of this, too, thou shalt have thy share, as is meet."

Then he went back to his tent, and set himself down, over against Priam, and spake: "Thy son is ransomed, old man, and to-morrow shalt thou see him and take him back to Troy. But now let us eat. Did not Niobe eat when she lost her twelve children, six daughters and six blooming sons, whom Apollo and Artemis slew — Apollo these and Artemis those — because she likened herself to the fair Latona?

So let us eat, old man. To-morrow shalt thou weep for Hector; many tears, I trow, shall be shed for him."

So they ate and drank. And when the meal was ended, Achilles sat and marvelled at King Priam's noble look, and King Priam marvelled at Achilles, so strong he was and fair.

Then Priam said: "Let me sleep, great Achilles. I have not slept since my son fell by thy hand. Now I have eaten and drunk, and my eyes are heavy."

So the comrades of Achilles made him a bed outside, where no one might see him, should it chance that any of the chiefs should come to the tent of Achilles to take counsel, and should espy him, and tell it to King Agamemnon.

But before he slept King Priam said: "If thou art minded to let me bury Hector, let there be a truce between my people and the Greeks. For nine days let us mourn for Hector, and on the tenth will we bury him and feast the people, and on the eleventh raise a great tomb above him, and on the twelfth we will fight again, if fight we must."

And Achilles answered, " Be it so: I will stay the war for so long."

But while Priam slept there came to him Hermes, the messenger of Zeus, and said: "Sleepest thou, Priam, among thy foes? Achilles has taken ransom for thy Hector; but thy sons that are left would pay thrice as much for thee should Agamemnon hear that thou wert among the ships."

The old man heard and trembled, and roused the herald, and the two yoked the horses and the mules. So they passed through the army, and no man knew. And when they came to the river, Hermes departed to Olympus, and the morning shone over all the earth. Wailing and weeping, they carried the body to the city.

It was Cassandra who first espied them as they came. Her father she saw, and the herald, and then the dead body on the litter, and she cried, "Sons and daughters of Troy, go to meet Hector, if ever ye have met him with joy as he came back from the battle."

And straightway there was not man or woman left in the city. They met the wagon when it was close to the gates : his wife led the way, and his mother and all the multitude followed. And in truth they would have kept it thus till evening, weeping and wailing, but King Priam spake : —

" Let us pass ; ye shall have enough of wailing when we have taken him to his home."

So they took him to his home and laid him on his bed. And the minstrels lamented, and the women wailed.

Then first of all came Andromaché, his wife, and cried : —

"O my husband, thou hast perished in thy youth, and I am left in widowhood, and our child, thy child and mine, is but an infant! I fear me he will not grow to manhood. Ere that day this city will fall, for thou art gone who wast its defender. Soon will they carry us away, mothers and children, in the ships, and thou, my son, perchance will be with us, and serve the stranger in unseemly bondage ; or, it may be, some Greek will slay thee, seizing thee and dashing thee from the wall ; some Greek whose brother, or father, or son, Hector has slain in the battle. Many a Greek did Hector slay; no gentle hand was his in the fray. There-fore, do the people wail for him to-day. Sore is thy parents' grief, O Hector, but sorest mine. Thou didst stretch no hands of farewell to me from thy bed, nor speak any word of comfort for me to muse on while I weep night and day."

Next spake Hecuba, his mother: "Dear wast thou, my son, in life to the immortal gods, and dear in death. Achilles dragged thee about the tomb of his dear Patroclus, but could not bring him back, I ween, and now thou liest fresh and fair as one whom the God of the silver bow has slain with sudden stroke."

And last of all came Helen, and cried: "Many a year has passed since I came to Troy—would that I had died before! And never have I heard from thy lips one bitter word, and if ever husband's sister, or sister-in-law, or mother-in-law—for Priam was ever gentle as a father—spake harshly to me, thou wouldst check them with thy grace and gracious words. Therefore I weep for thee; no one is left to be my friend in all the broad streets of Troy. All shun and hate me now."

And all the people wailed reply.

Then Priam spake: "Go, my people, gather wood for the burial, and fear not any ambush of the Greeks, for Achilles promised that he would stay the war until the twelfth day should come."

So for nine days the people gathered much wood, and on the tenth they laid Hector upon the pile, and lit fire beneath it. And when it was burnt they quenched the embers with wine. Then his brethren and comrades gathered together the white bones, and laid them in a chest of gold; and this they covered with purple robes and put in a great coffin, and laid upon it stones many and great. And over all they raised a mighty mound; and all the while the watchers watched, lest the Greeks should arise and slay them. Last of all was a great feast held in the palace of King Priam.

So they buried Hector, the tamer of horses.

---

### THE END OF TROY.

After these things came Memnon the Æthiopian to the help of Troy. He slew Antilochus, son of Nestor, in battle, but was himself slain by Achilles. Not many days after this Achilles himself perished, for, having declared at a banquet of the chiefs that he would make his way by his valour into Troy, he strove to break through the Scæan gate. There did Paris wound him to the death with an arrow, but it was Apollo that guided the archer's hand.

When Achilles was dead, his mother gave his arms to be a prize to the bravest of the Greeks. Then stood up Ulysses and Ajax the Greater, and contended together; but the Greeks adjudged the prize to Ulysses; therefore Ajax slew himself.

Yet still Troy could not be taken. Then Helenus the seer, who was one of the sons of Priam, having been taken prisoner by Ulysses, said to the Greeks: "Ye cannot take the city unless ye bring hither Philoctetes, with the bow which Hercules gave him, and with him one who is one of the race of Achilles."

Now the Greeks, when they sailed to Troy, had left Philoctetes in Lemnos, because the stench of the wound where a serpent had bitten him could not be endured. So they sent Ulysses to fetch him. Also they sent for Neoptolemus, the son of Achilles, that was brought up in Scyros by the father of his mother.

Philoctetes, when he was come to Troy, slew Paris with one of the arrows of Hercules, and Neoptolemus slew the son of Telephus, who was the last and bravest of the allies of Troy.

But when the city still held out, a certain Epeius, Athené advising him, devised a device by which it was taken. The Greeks made as if they had departed, burning their camp and sailing away in their ships. But they left behind them a great horse of wood in which the bravest of the chiefs hid themselves. This the men of Troy drew into their city; and at night, when their thoughts were given to feasting, for they thought that the war was ended, the chiefs came out of the horse and threw open the gate, so that the Greeks entered and took the city.

COLSTON AND COMPANY, LTD., PRINTERS, EDINBURGH.